The
Schwa
was
Here

Neal Shusterman

The Schwa was Here

SCHOLASTIC INC.

New York   Toronto   London   Auckland   Sydney
Mexico City   New Delhi   Hong Kong   Buenos Aires

ISBN-13: 978-0-439-90223-6
ISBN-10: 0-439-90223-1

12 11 10 9 8 7   15 16/0

Printed in the U.S.A.   40

First Scholastic printing, September 2006

Designed by Heather Wood

Lexile is a registered trademark of MetaMetrics, Inc.

For my grandparents Gussie and Dave Altman,
who will always be the spirit of Brooklyn to me

schwa: The faint vowel sound in many unstressed syllables in the English language. It is signified by the pronunciation "uh" and represented by the symbol ə. For example, the *e* in *overlook*, the *a* in *forgettable*, and the *o* in *run-of-the-mill*.

It is the most common vowel sound in the English language.

Manny Bullpucky Gets His Sorry Butt Hurled Off the Marine Park Bridge

1 I don't really remember when I first met the Schwa, he was just kind of always there, like the killer potholes on Avenue U or the Afghans barking out the windows above Crawley's restaurant—a whole truck load of 'em, if you believed the rumors. Old Man Crawley, by the way, was a certifiable loony tune. A shut-in, like Brooklyn's own Howard Hughes, almost as legendary as the lobsters served up in his restaurant below. See, there was this staircase that went up from the restaurant to the residence on the second floor, but with each step it got darker around you, so when you tried to climb it, you kept thinking you heard the horror audience behind you yelling, "No, don't go up the stairs!" Because who but a moron would go up to search for Old Man Crawley, who had fingernails like Ginsu knives that could dice, slice, and julienne you, then serve you up in like fourteen thousand plastic dog bowls. Those bowls, by the way, would probably be made by my father, the Vice-Executive Vice-Vice-President of Product

Development for Pisher Plastic Products. If you're a guy, I'm sure you already know that their most famous product is that little plastic strainer at the bottom of urinals, and you probably still laugh every time you look down while taking a leak and see PISHER® written in happy bold letters, like maybe it was to remind you why you were standing there.

But what was I talking about?

Oh, yeah—the Schwa. See, that was the whole point with the Schwa: You couldn't even think about him without losing track of your own thoughts—like even in your head he was somehow becoming invisible.

Okay, so like I said, I don't remember when I met him—nobody does—but I can tell you the first time I remembered actually noticing him. It was the day Manny Bullpucky jumped from the Marine Park Bridge.

It was a Saturday, and my friends and I were bored, as usual. I was hanging out with Howie Bogerton, whose one goal in life was not to have any goals in life, and Ira Goldfarb, who was a self-proclaimed cinematic genius. With the digital video camera his grandparents had gotten him for his bar mitzvah last year, Ira was determined to be Steven Spielberg by the time he got to high school. As for Manny Bullpucky, we kinda dragged him along with us to various places we went. We had to drag him around, on accounta he was a dummy. Not a dummy like Wendell Tiggor, who had to repeat the fifth grade like fourteen thousand times, but a real dummy. More snooty people might call him a mannequin, or even a *prosthetic personage,* because nobody calls things what they really are anymore. But to us normal people in Gerritsen Beach, Brooklyn, he was a dummy, plain and simple.

As for his name, it came in the natural course of human events. Dad had brought him home from work one day. "Look at this guy," he says proudly, holding him up by the scruff of his neck. "He's made of a new ultra-high-grade lightweight plastic. Completely unbreakable."

My older brother Frank looks up from his dinner. "Bull-pucky," he says—although I'm editing out the bad word here, on accounta my mother might read this, and I don't like the taste of soap.

As soon as Frankie says it, Mom, without missing a beat, hauls off and whacks him on the head in her own special way, starting low, and swinging up, like a tennis player giving a ball topspin, just grazing the thin spot on his head that's gonna be bald someday, probably from Mom slapping him there. "You watch ya mout!" Mom says. "Mout," not "mouth." We got a problem here with the "th" sound. It's not just us—it's all a Brooklyn, maybe Queens, too. My English teacher says I also drop vowels like a bad juggler, and have an infuriating tense problem, whatever that meant. So anyway, if you put the "th" problem and the vowel thing together, our family's Catlick, in-stead of Catholic, and my name's Antny instead of Anthony. Somehow that got changed into Antsy when I was little, and they've called me Antsy ever since. It don't bother me no more. Used to, but, y'know, you grow into your name.

Anyway, Dad tosses me the dummy. "Here, take it," he says.

"Whadaya giving it to me for?"

"Why do you think? I want you to break it."

"I thought you said it was unbreakable."

"Yeah, and you're the test, *capische?*"

I smile, proud to figure in my father's product development

job. This was the first time in recorded history that either of my parents had singled me out to do anything.

"Do I get to break something?" my little sister Christina asks.

"Yeah," says Dad. "Wait a few years and you'll be breaking hearts."

Christina must have liked the sound of that, because she flips open the journal that's practically glued to her hand and makes a note of it.

So Howie, Ira, and me, we started doin' unpleasant things to Manny that might break him. Ira loves this, because he can get the whole thing on film. We rode our bikes down Flatbush Avenue to the Marine Park Bridge, which is no easy task considering I gotta carry Manny on my handlebars. God forbid Frankie, who just got his license, could give us a ride in the old Toyota he just got. No, he's too busy hanging out with all the other perfect people—but don't get me started on Frankie.

We got to the bridge, and the three of us, not including Manny, worked out our game plan.

"I should go down to the rocks to film," Ira said. "I'll get a good view of him falling from there."

"Nah," says Howie, "let's go to the middle of the bridge—I wanna see him hit the water."

"If he hits the water," I reminded them, "we won't get him back."

Howie shrugs. "There's lots of boats goin' by, maybe we can time it so he hits a boat."

"We still won't get him back," I said, "and we might sink the boat."

"That'd look good on film," Ira said.

Now all this time I got this creepy feeling like we're being watched. But then of course we *are* being watched. Everybody driving by has got to be wondering what we're doing standing with a dummy by the guardrail of the bridge—but this feeling is more than that. Anyway, I ignore the feeling because we had important business here.

"We'll drop him onto the rocks," I told them.

"Yeah," says Howie. "Maximum breakage potential."

"Great. Howie, you stay up here on the bridge to push him over; Ira and me'll go down and watch."

We climbed down to the rocks and looked up to where Howie stood holding Manny by the scruff of the neck—it's a pretty high drop. I didn't envy Manny. Still that feeling of being watched just won't go away.

"Should I push him or should I throw him?" Howie asks.

"Do what comes naturally," I yelled back.

"I don't know," he says. "This is a very unnatural thing."

"Rolling," says Ira. " And . . . action."

Howie backs up for a second, and a moment later Manny Bullpucky comes hurtling over the side of the bridge, arms and legs flailing like he's really alive, and he does a swan dive headfirst toward the rocks. *WHAM!* He hits the jagged boulders, and it's all over for him. His bald head goes flying like a cannonball shot straight at me. I hit the deck, narrowly miss being decapitated, and when I get up again, a headless mannequin lies with his arms strewn on the rocks, just another casualty of the fast life.

Howie comes running down from the bridge.

"What happened? Did he break? Did he break?"

"Yeah," I told him, picking myself off of the ground. "We're gonna have to change his name to 'Headless Joe.'"

Ira, still behind the camera, moved in closer to the body, paused dramatically, and finally stopped filming. "Where'd his head go?"

I shrugged. "I don't know, over there somewhere. So much for unbreakable plastic."

"Are you looking for this?" I heard another voice say. The voice was scratchy, like a kid who's screamed a little too much. I turned, and I swear to you, the first thing I see is Manny's mannequin head floating in midair. I only see it for a split second, but it's the creepiest thing. Then in that split second my brain does a quick retake and I see that there's a kid holding the head under his armpit. I couldn't really see the kid at first on accounta his clothes are kind of a brownish gray, like the rocks around him, and you know how your mind can play tricks on you when the light is just right.

"Excuse me," said Ira, "this is a closed set."

The kid ignored him. "That was pretty cool," he said. "You should have dressed him up, though, so when he fell he looked like a person and not a dummy on film."

Ira pursed his lips and got a little red, annoyed that he didn't think of it.

"Don't I know you?" I asked the kid. I took a good look at him. His hair was kinda ashen blond—real wispy, like if you held a magnetized balloon over his head, all his hair would stand on end. He was about a head shorter than me; a little too thin. Other than that, there was nothing remarkable about him, nothing at all. He wasn't good-looking; he wasn't ugly; he wasn't buff and he wasn't scrawny. He was just, like, average. Like if you looked up "kid" in the dictionary, his face would be there.

"I'm in some class with you, right?" I asked him.

"Science," he said. "I sit next to you in science class."

"Oh yeah, that's right, now I remember." Although for the life of me I have no memory of him sitting next to me.

"I'm Calvin," he said. "Calvin Schwa."

With that Ira gasped, "You're the kid they call the Schwa?"

"Yeah, I guess."

Ira took a step back.

"I'm Anthony Bonano," I told him, "but everyone calls me Antsy. These are my friends Howie and Ira." Then I pointed to the head in his hands. "You already met Manny."

He took Manny's head back to his body. "So what's all this for, anyway?"

"Pisher Plastics product stress test," I told him, trying to sound professional.

"Manny gets an F," Howie said. "He's supposed to be unbreakable."

"Technology fails again," I said, all the while noticing how Ira still kept his distance from the Schwa, as if he were radioactive, like some of those flounder they found off Canarsie Pier.

The Schwa knelt next to Manny's headless body.

"Technically he's not broken," the Schwa said.

"If your head comes off, you're broken," says Howie. "Trust me."

"See? Look here." He pointed to the neck. "His head is held on by a ball-and-socket joint. It just popped off—watch." Then the Schwa snapped Manny's head back on as if it were a giant Barbie. I was both relieved and disappointed. It was good to know my dad's work was successful, but upsetting to know that I couldn't destroy it.

"So what do we do to him next?" Howie asked.

"Pyrotechnics," said Ira. "We try to blow him up."

"Can I come, too?" asked the Schwa.

"Yeah, sure, why not?" I turned to him, but he's gone. "Hey, where'd ya go?"

"I'm right here."

I squinted to get the sun out of my eyes, and I saw him. He's waving his hands, like to get my attention or something.

"I don't know," said Ira. "You know what they say about too many cooks."

"No, what?" asks Howie.

"You know—too many cooks stink up the kitchen."

Howie *still* looks confused. "What, don't these cooks know from deodorant?"

"It's an expression, Howie," I explained. Howie, you gotta understand, ain't dumb. He just doesn't think out of the box. Of course, if I ever told him that, he'd wonder what box I was talking about. He's the kinda guy who's hardwired to take everything literally. Which is why he's so good at math and science, but when it comes to anything creative—he tanks. He's about as creative as a bar code. Even when he was little, he would do real good at coloring when there were nice thick black lines in the coloring book—but give him some crayons and a blank page, and his forehead would start to bleed. So, anyways, by a two-to-one vote the Schwa is allowed to join us in our next attempt to bust Manny. Ira voted no, but he wouldn't look at any of us when he did.

"So what's up with you?" I asked him.

"It's my opinion. I got a right to an opinion."

"Okay, okay, don't get so touchy."

With Ira suddenly unsociable, the Schwa decided to leave rather than make any further waves.

"See you in science," he said.

Only after he's gone does Ira pull me aside and say, "I wish I would've gotten *that* on film."

"Gotten what on film?"

"Remember a second ago when you asked the Schwa where he went, and he practically had to jump up and down to get your attention?"

"Yeah?"

"He was standing right in front of you all along."

I waved my hand like I'm shooing away a fly. "What are you talking about? He moved behind me. That's why I couldn't see him."

But Howie shook his head. "He never moved, Antsy."

I scowled at them like this is some conspiracy to make me look stupid.

"And I've heard things about him, too," Ira said. "Crazy stuff."

"Such as?"

Ira came in close enough so I could smell last night's garlic-whatever on his breath. "His eyes," Ira whispered. "They say his eyes change color to match the sky. They say his shoes are always the same color as the ground. They say if you stare at him long enough, you can read what's written on the wall behind him."

"That's called 'persistence of vision,'" Howie says, reminding us that behind his veil of idiocy is a keen analytical mind. "That's when your brain fills in the gaps of what it thinks ought to be there."

"He's not a gap," I reminded him. "He's a kid."

"He's a freak," said Ira. "Ten-foot-pole material."

Well, I didn't know about Howie and Ira, but I've spent enough of my life keeping weird things at ten-foot-pole distance.

"If any of this is true," I told them, "there are ways of finding out."

The Weird and Mostly Tragic History
of the Schwa, Which Is Entirely True
If You Trust My Sources

2 My family lives in a duplex—that's two homes attached like Siamese twins with one wall in common. On the other side of the wall is a Jewish family. Ira knows them from his temple, but we just know their names. Once a year we exchange Christmas cookies and potato latkes. Funny how you can live six inches away from people and barely even know them. Our neighborhood is a Jewish-Italian neighborhood. Jews and Italians seem to get along just fine. I think it has something to do with the way both cultures have a high regard for food and guilt.

The Schwa was about six inches away, too, in science class, but I had never noticed him. It was weird, because in school I notice almost anything as long as it doesn't actually have to do with the lesson. And then there was the way Ira got all freaked out about him. It made me want to do some investigating. It took a couple of days, but I did come up with something.

I called Ira and Howie over for a war council, which I guess is the guy version of gossiping. Of course we couldn't talk in the living room, because Frankie was sleeping on the sofa, hogging the most comfortable place in the house, like always. Lately it's like Frankie slept all the time.

"It comes with being sixteen," Mom said. "You teenagers, you go into a cocoon when you turn fifteen and don't come out for years."

"So they become butterflies when they finally come out?" my little sister Christina asked.

"No," Mom said. "They're still caterpillars, only now they're big fat caterpillars that smell."

Christina laughed and Frankie rolled over on the sofa, sticking his butt out toward us.

"So when do we get to be butterflies?" I asked.

"You don't," Mom answered. "You go off to college, or wherever, and then *I* get to be a butterfly."

She was looking at me when she said "wherever," so I said, "Maybe I'll just stay here all my life. With a butterfly net."

"Yeah," said Mom. "Then you can use it to drag me off to the nuthouse."

When it comes to Frankie, Mom always talks about college like it's a given, but not me. I looked at Frankie snoring away. Sometimes I think God made an inventory error and gave Frankie some brain cells that were supposed to go to me. He could sleep away the afternoon and still pull straight A's, but me? There were only two A's I ever saw on my papers: the *A* in *Anthony*, and the *A* in *Bonano*. What made it worse was that Christina already seemed to be following in Frankie's footsteps, gradewise, so it cleared the path for me to be the family disappointment.

"C'mon," I told Howie and Ira, "we'll talk in the basement," which is the place we always talk about important things. Ours is what you call a finished basement, although it really should be called a someday-will-be-finished basement, because no matter how much work we put into it, there always seems to be a bare wall with insulation that's never been covered up. It probably has something to do with my dad, who keeps putting in the wrong wiring, or my uncle, who got cheap insulation that just happens to cause cancer. Whatever the reason, walls keep having to come out. Still, the basement had become like our own military bunker where we discuss national security and play video games that my mother is convinced will rot out my brain even faster than professional wrestling. And it really pisses her off when we play the wrestling video game.

But today we're not playing games. Today is a war council about the weird kid everyone calls the Schwa.

We sat on the floor, and I told them what I found out in the course of my investigation. "I'm not a hundred percent sure how the Schwa got his last name, but my aunt's hairdresser's brother is his next-door neighbor, so the story must be pretty reliable." I paused for effect. "The story goes like this: The Schwa's great-grandparents came over from the old country."

"Which old country?" asked Howie.

"I don't know, one of those old countries over there."

"China's an old country," says Howie. "He doesn't look Chinese."

Now I know why Howie always buzzes his hair, because if he didn't, he'd have millions of people trying to pull it out.

"He means somewhere in Eastern Europe," Ira said.

"Anyway," I said, "his great-grandfather's last name is Schwartz, and for his whole life, all Great-Grandpa Schwartz wants to do is to get out of the old country and come to America, because the Statue of Liberty's got this invitation: 'Give me your tired, your poor, your reeking homeless—"

"'Huddled masses,'" said Ira. "'Give me your tired, your poor, your huddled masses yearning to breathe free.'"

"Yeah," says Howie. "If you're gonna misquote something, at least misquote it right."

"Okay, fine. So, like everybody in the old countries says, 'Hey, I'm a huddled mass,' and they all wanna come over. That's how come my great-grandparents came from Italy, and why Ira's came from Russia, and why yours, Howie, came from the moon." Howie punched me in the arm for that one.

"So, anyway, Old Man Schwartz, he's stewing out there on his beet farm, or whatever, saving his pennies to buy a ticket for himself and his wife and kids so he can take a boat to America. 'I want to die on American soil,' he says. Finally he saves up enough money, and they pack 'em onto a boat with like, fourteen thousand other families, and they cross the Atlantic Ocean."

"Don't tell me they hit an iceberg," says Howie.

"Different boat," I said, "but around the same time, I guess. Anyway, they get into New York Harbor, pass the Statue of Liberty, everybody starin' up at the flame going ooh and ahh like tourists without Hawaiian shirts—because, you know, they're poor, they can't afford Hawaiian shirts. Anyway, they let everyone off the boat at Ellis Island and they get in this long line standing in the hot sun, all sweaty in heavy coats, because these people don't yet know to dress for the weather, because it's always subzero in the old country. Finally they get to the front of the line. Old Man Schwartz, he's sweating from the heat, and hyperventilating from the excitement. There's this guy in the front of the line with a fountain pen and a big, fat black book taking down names and letting you into the country. He says, 'Your name, sir?' And—get this—the old man says, 'Schwa—,' then puts his hand over his heart, has a massive heart attack, and drops dead on the spot."

"He got his wish," says Howie. "He died on American soil."

"Yeah. So anyway, those guys at Ellis Island, they were like your cafeteria workers of today—they didn't care what they stuck you with, as long as they got you through the line. So they marked down the family name as 'Schwa,' and it's been that way ever since."

Ira, who had been quiet for most of the story, finally spoke up. "That's not all I heard."

I turned to him. "What'd you hear?"

"Weird stuff—not just about him this time, but about the whole family."

"Weird, like *Twilight Zone* weird?" Howie asked. "Or weird like *Eyewitness News* weird?"

"I don't know," said Ira. "Maybe a little bit of both."

"So what did you hear?" I asked again.

"I heard his mom went to the market one day and disappeared right before everyone's eyes in the ten-items-or-less line. Nothing was left but a pile of coupons and a broken jar of pickles where she stood."

"Disappeared? What do you mean disappeared?"

"And why a pile of coupons, if all she had was a jar of pickles?" Howie asked.

"It's just what I heard." Then Ira gets real quiet. "Of course . . . there's another story."

Howie and I leaned close to listen.

"Some say the Schwa's father cut her up into fifty pieces and mailed each piece . . . to a PO box . . . in a different state . . ."

"Not Puerto Rico?" says Howie.

"Puerto Rico's not a state," I reminded him.

"It's almost a state."

"Fine, so maybe he saved a piece to send to Puerto Rico when it becomes a state. Okay, are you happy?"

To tell you the truth, I didn't believe either of Ira's stories. "If any of this stuff happened, the whole neighborhood would know about it—wouldn't they?"

Ira leaned in close and smirked. "Not if it happened before he moved here."

"When did he move here?" asked Howie.

But neither Ira or I knew for sure. The thing is, there are always kids moving in and out of neighborhoods, and no matter how quietly a kid tries to come into a new school, he can't do it without being noticed. But the Schwa did.

"I guess he kinda slipped in under everybody's radar," I said.

"Has anyone bothered to check if the color of his eyes really changes?" Howie asked.

"I don't want to get that close," said Ira.

There was silence for a second, and then Howie let off a shiver that I could feel like a tremor.

Quantizing the Schwa Effect
Using the Scientific Method,
and All That Garbage

3 Mr. Werthog, our science teacher, has a weird twitch in his lip, like he's always kissing the air. It's something you never can get used to, and might explain why my science grade keeps dropping. You just can't concentrate on his words when you look at him. The only time it gets him into trouble, though, is during parent conference night. One guy punched him out for making kissy faces at his wife.

Now he stood in front of a science experiment featuring a large beaker filled with ice and a long thermometer. On the board he writes 34°, then turned to us. "The scientific method *(kiss)* is one of hypothesis, trial *(kiss)*, results, and conclusion *(kiss, kiss)*."

Someone next to me taps my arm. "Hi, Antsy."

I turn, actually surprised to see someone there. It's like I never realized there was even a desk next to me in science. For an instant I don't recognize the face—like no part of it is distinctive enough to stick to my memory—a face like mental Teflon.

"It's me—Calvin Schwa."

"Hey, Schwa—how ya doin?"

"Mr. Bonano, are you *(kiss)* with us today?"

"Uh . . . yeah, I guess." I don't kiss back, on account of I once got dragged to the office for that. Mr. Werthog is sensitive that way.

"As I was saying, *(kiss)* can anyone give me the hypothesis leading to today's experiment?"

The Schwa's hand is up in an instant, before anyone else's. We're in the third row, right in the middle, but Werthog looks over his hand to Amy van Zandt, in the last row.

"Water at room temperature will boil if left in the sun."

"Abominably incorrect!" He pours a packet of powder into the icy beaker, and stirs it. The water turns cloudly. "Anyone else?"

The Schwa's hand is still up. Werthog calls on LoQuisha Peel.

"Lemonade reacts with ice to quench thirst?" LoQuisha says.

"Even more wrong *(kiss, kiss)*." He pours in a second packet of powder. The ice in the beaker begins to melt quickly. By now the Schwa is waving his hand back and forth across Werthog's field of vision like a signal flare. Werthog calls on Dennis Fiorello.

"Uh . . ." Dennis puts down his hand. "Never mind."

The Schwa turns to me, grumbling beneath his breath. "He never calls on me."

That's when I raise my hand.

"Ah! Mr. Bonano. Do you have the answer?"

"No, but I'll bet the Schwa does."

He looks at me like I'm speaking Latin. "Excuse me?"

"You know: Calvin Schwa."

Werthog turns his head slightly and his eyes refocus. "Calvin!" he says, like he's surprised he's even here. "Can you *(kiss)* give us the answer?"

"The reaction between reagents A and B is an exothermic reaction."

"Excellent! And is our hypothesis proven, or disproven?"

"Proven. All the ice melted when you added reagent B, so it's exothermic."

Werthog pulls out the thermometer, marks down the temperature on the board, 89°, and continues his lesson.

The Schwa turns to me and whispers, "Thanks. At least now he won't mark me absent today."

I shake my head and laugh. "I swear, it's like you're invisible or something." I say it like a joke, but then I catch the Schwa's eyes—eyes that match the gray clouds outside the window. He doesn't say anything, and I know I just stumbled onto something. He turns back to his notebook, but I can't concentrate on my work. I feel like my foot is pressed down on a land mine that will blow the second I move.

Howie, Ira, and I got together the next Saturday morning to detonate Manny. I had told the Schwa about it the day before, but in a way I was hoping he wouldn't show—almost as much as I hoped he would. I call it the "film-at-eleven factor." You know, on the news, how they say, "Horrible train wreck. Graphic footage. Film at eleven." And then for the rest of the night you're disgusted by how much you actually want to see it, and you're relieved if you fall asleep before it comes on.

The thing is, I can't get past the feeling that there's something . . . unnatural about the Schwa. I don't do well with un-natural things. Take spiders, for instance. I mean, sorry, I don't care what anyone says—there can't be anything natural about spinning a web out of your butt. And then there's those Hindu coal walkers. The way I see it, if God meant us to walk on hot coals, He would have given us asbestos hooves instead of feet—but first He probably would have smashed us in the head a couple of times to knock some sense into us, because why would we want to walk on coals in the first place? And don't even get me started on my aunt Rose's Christmas tree. First of all, it's aluminum. Second of all, it's pink. I mean, like the color of Pepto-Bismol, which makes sense, because I get sick to my stomach just looking at it.

Not that the Schwa is anything like a spider, or a coal walker, or a pink tree, but he is unnatural in his own disturbing Schwa-like way.

So anyway, it's seven on Saturday morning as we prepare Manny Bullpucky for detonation. I'm busy taping an M-80 firecracker to his forehead, but my mind's obviously not on my work because I bury the whole fuse beneath the duct tape.

"You're a real pyrotechnic wizard, Antsy," says Ira as he pulls off the tape and redoes it.

Behind me, Howie's upturning lawn furniture, building a barricade for us to hide behind when Manny blows.

"I've been thinking about the Schwa," I said, loud enough for both Howie and Ira to hear.

"Yeah, so?" said Ira.

"I've been thinking there's something wrong with him."

"Like he's retarded, you mean?"

Howie's disgusted by this. "The proper term is 'mentally handicapped,'" he says. "Otherwise retards get offended."

"No," I tell them. "The Schwa's not mentally handicapped—it's something else—and don't pretend you don't know what I'm talking about."

"Hey, didn't I say there was something weird about him?" Ira said. "I mean, like the way he always just appears, like he's spying on you. He's sneaky. Weaselly . . ."

"I don't think he means to be," I told them. "It's just . . . It's just like he always happens to be standing in your blind spot."

"Yeah, and when he's around, every spot is a blind spot," said Ira. "It's friggin' weird. It's like he's a ghost, or something."

"You gotta be dead to be a ghost," I reminded him. "No . . . It's more like he's . . ." I search for the right word. "It's like he's *functionally invisible.*"

"The proper term is 'observationally challenged,'" Howie says.

"Whadaya mean 'proper term'? How can there be a proper term for it when I just made it up?"

"Well, if you're gonna make something up, make up the proper term."

I keep trying to think this through. "It's like when he's in a room and doesn't say anything, you could walk in, walk out, and never know he was there."

"Like the tree falling in the forest," says Ira.

"Huh?"

"You know, it's the old question—if a tree falls in a forest and no one's there to hear it, does it really make a sound?"

Howie considers this. "Is it a pine forest, or oak?"

"What's the difference?"

"Oak is a much denser wood; it's more likely to be heard by someone on the freeway next to the forest where no one is."

I know I'm in over my head here, because Howie's logic is actually starting to make sense. "What does a tree in the forest have to do with the Schwa?" I ask Ira.

And the Schwa says, "I know."

We snapped our heads around so sharply, it's like whiplash. The Schwa was there, leaning up against my backyard fence! It's like we're all too dumbfounded to speak.

"I know what it has to do with me," he said. "I'm like that tree. If I stand in a room and no one sees me, it's like I was never there at all. Sometimes I even wonder if I was there myself."

"Wh-when did you get here?" I asked him.

"I got here before Howie and Ira did. I was hoping you'd notice. You didn't."

"So . . . you heard everything?"

He nodded. I tried to run the whole conversation through my mind, to see if I had said anything bad about him. His feelings didn't appear hurt, though—like he was used to people talking behind his back in front of his face.

"I've wondered about it myself," he said. "You know—being observationally challenged . . . functionally invisible." He paused for a second, then looked at Manny all strung up like a scarecrow. "You ought to find a seam in the plastic, and tape the M-80 there."

"Huh?" It took a few seconds for me to drag my mind back to the reason why we were all here. "Oh! Right." I went to Manny, pulled off the duct tape, and felt around his bald head for the plastic seam. I retaped the fat firecracker on the back of his head, relieved not to have to look at the Schwa. Ira fiddled with his camera, and Howie finished up our protective barricade.

"How long will it take the fuse to burn?" I asked, as illegal fireworks are not my particular academic strength.

"Twelve point five seconds," says Howie. "But that's just an estimate."

We let the Schwa light the fuse, as he seemed to be the only one not afraid of blowing up, and he quickly joined us behind the barricade.

"You know, there's gotta be a way to quantify it," Howie says while we wait for the fuse to burn down.

"What?"

"The Schwa Effect. It's like Mr. Werthog says: 'For an experiment to be valid, the results must be quantifiable and repeatable *(kiss, kiss).*'"

"We should experiment on the Schwa?"

"Sounds good to me," said the Schwa.

Then a blast knocks me to the ground. My ears pop and begin to ring. The blast echoes back and forth down the row of brick duplexes. When I look up, Manny's body has flown six feet, and his head is gone again.

Ira zoomed in on the body. "Thus perished Manny Bullpucky." He turned the camera off. Right about now every window in Brooklyn is snapping up as people wonder what morons are setting off fireworks at seven in the morning.

We hurry inside so we don't get caught. Once we're in, I look at the Schwa. "After that, you really want us to experiment on you?"

"Sure," he says. "What's life without excitement?"

I had to hand it to the Schwa. Any other kid would have flipped us off if asked to be a lab rat, but the Schwa was a good sport. Maybe he was just as curious about his own weirdness as we were.

———

LAB JOURNAL
The Schwa Effect: Experiment #1

Hypothesis: The Schwa will be functionally invisible in your standard classroom.

Materials: Nine random students, one classroom, the Schwa.

Procedure: We set nine students and the Schwa seated around an otherwise empty classroom (if you don't count the hamsters and the guinea pig in the back). Then we dragged other students into the room, and asked them to do a head count.

Results: Three out of five students refused to go into the classroom on account of they thought there'd be a bucket of water over the door, or something nasty like that, which is understandable because we've been known to play practical, and less practical, jokes. Eventually we managed to round up twenty students to go into the room, count the people in the room, then report back to us. Fifteen students said that there were nine people in the room. Four students said there were ten. One student said there were seventeen (we believe he counted the hamsters and guinea pig).

Conclusion: Four out of five people do not see the Schwa in your standard classroom.

I don't know what it was about the Schwa that kept getting to me. I can't say I was always thinking about him—I mean, he was hard to think about—that was part of the problem. You start to think about him and pretty soon you find yourself thinking about a video game, or last Christmas, or fourteen thousand other things, and you can't remember what you were thinking about in the first place. It's like your brain begins to twist and squirm, directing your mind away from him. Of course that's nothing new to me—I mean, it seems like my brain is always twitching in unexpected directions, especially when there are girls around. I've never been the smoothest guy around girls that I like. I'll say stupid things, like pointing out they got mud on their shoes or mustard on the tip of their nose, like Mary Ellen MacCaw did once—but with a schnoz like hers, it's hard not to get condiments on it, and maybe even a condiment bottle lodged up inside there once in a while. My awkwardness with girls did change, though, once I met Lexie. Lots of things changed after I met Lexie—but wait a second, I'm getting way ahead of myself here. What was I talking about? Oh yeah. The Schwa.

See? You start thinking about the Schwa, and you end up thinking about everything but. I guess this fascination I had with the Schwa was because in some small way I knew how he felt. See, I never stand out in a crowd either. I'm just your run-of-the-mill eighth-grade wiseass, which might get me somewhere in, like, Iowa, but Brooklyn is wiseass central. No one ever has anything major to say about me, good or bad, and even in my own family, I'm kind of just "there." Frankie's God's gift to Brooklyn, Christina gets all the attention because she's the youngest, and me, well, I'm like an afterthought. "You've got middle-child syndrome," I've been told. Well, seems to me more like middle-finger syndrome. Do you ever sit and play that game where you try to imagine yourself in the future? Well, whenever *I* try to imagine my future, all I can see are my classmates twenty years from now asking one another, "Hey, whatever happened to Antsy Bonano?" And even in that weird little daydream no one had a clue. But the Schwa—he was worse off than me. He wouldn't be the "whatever-happened-to" kid—he'd be the kid whose picture gets accidentally left out of the yearbook and no one notices. Although I'm a bit ashamed to say it, it felt good to be around someone more invisible than me.

LAB JOURNAL
The Schwa Effect: Experiment #2

Hypothesis: The Schwa will not be noticed even when dressed weird and acting freakishly.

Materials: The boys' bathroom, a sombrero spray-painted Day-Glo orange, a costume from last year's school production of *Cats,* and the Schwa.

Procedure: The Schwa was asked to stand in the middle of the boys' bathroom wearing the cat costume and the orange sombrero, and to sing "God Bless America" at the top of his lungs. We ask unsuspecting students coming out of the bathroom if they noticed anything unusual in there.

Results: We caught fifteen people willing to discuss their lavatory experience. When asked if there was anything strange going on, aside from the one kid who kept talking about a toilet that wouldn't stop flushing, fourteen out of fifteen said there was someone acting weird in the bathroom. We thought the experiment was a failure until we asked them to describe the weirdo.

"He was wearing something strange, I think," one person said.

"He wore like a pointed blue party hat, I think," said another.

Not a single person identified the orange sombrero, or the cat costume, although one person was reasonably certain that he had a tail.

All agreed that he was singing something patriotic, but no one could remember what it was. Five people were sure it was "The Star-Spangled Banner." Six people said it was "My Country 'Tis of

Thee." Only four properly identified it as "God Bless America."

Conclusion: Even when acting weird and dressed like a total freak, the Schwa is only barely noticed.

———

The basketball courts in our neighborhood parks have steel chain-link nets. I like that better than regular string net because when you make a basket, you don't *swish*—you *clank*. That heavy, hearty rattle is more satisfying. More macho than a swish. It's powerful, like the roar of a crowd—something invisible kids like the Schwa and semi-invisible kids like me never get to hear except in our own heads.

It was on the basketball court that I came up with the Big Idea.

By now the Schwa was hanging around with us more—I mean when we actually noticed him there. Ira was not too thrilled about it. See, Ira was not invisible. He had made great advances into the visible world. Take his video camera for instance. You'd think it would make him a behind-the-scenes type of guy. Not so—because when Ira has his eye to the viewfinder, he becomes the center of attention. He directs the world, and the world allows it. So I guess I could see why he kept his distance from the Schwa. Invisibility threatened him.

Ira did join us on the basketball court, though. Couldn't resist that, I guess, and in playing "friendly" choose-up games, we had quickly learned how to turn the Schwa Effect to our advantage.

Move number one: Fake to the left, pass right to the Schwa, shoot, score!

"Hey—where did *he* come from?" someone on the other team would always yell.

Move number two: Dribble up the middle, flip it back to the Schwa, who'd drive down the sidelines for a layup—shoot—score!

"What?! Who's guarding that guy?" It was great watching the other teams get all frustrated, never noticing the Schwa until the ball was already in his hands.

Move number three: Pass to Howie, back to me, and then to the Schwa, who's right under the basket. A quick hook shot—score!

As for the other team, there would be much weeping and gnashing of teeth, as the Bible says.

On this particular day, after the other kids went off to console themselves in their humiliating loss, Howie, the Schwa, and I hung around on the court just shooting around. Ira also left right after the game, not wanting to hang around the Schwa any longer than he had to.

"We oughta go out for the team," Howie suggested as we shot baskets. "We've got a system."

"The Schwa oughta go out for the team, you mean," I said.

The Schwa dribbled the ball a bit, took a hook shot, and sunk it. "I played peewee basketball a few years back, but it didn't work out."

"Don't tell me—the coach always forgot to put you in, and even when you were in, nobody passed to you."

He shrugs like it's a given. "My father never showed up for the games either. So I figured, what was the point?"

"How about your mother?" says Howie. I might be the prince of foot-in-mouth disease, but Howie's the king. He grimaces the moment after he says it, but it's already out.

The Schwa doesn't say anything at first. He takes another shot. He misses. "My mother's not around anymore."

Howie keeps looking at me, like I'm gonna cough up the guts to ask about it, but I won't do it. I mean, what am I supposed to say? "Is it true that your mom was abducted by aliens in the middle of Waldbaum's supermarket?" or "Is it true your father got a samurai sword and went Benihana on her?"

No. Instead I change the subject, changing all of our lives from that moment on, because that's when I come up with what would forever be known as Stealth Economics.

"Hey, if the Schwa Effect works on the basketball court, there's got to be other ways to put it to good use."

The Schwa stopped dribbling. "Like how?"

"I don't know . . . Spy on people and stuff."

Howie's ears perked up at the mention of spy stuff. "The government would pay big bucks for someone who's invisible."

"He's not invisible," I reminded him. "He's *invisible-ish*. Like a stealth fighter."

"The CIA could still use him."

"And abuse him." I grabbed the ball away from the Schwa, went in for a layup, and made it.

"I don't want to go to the government," the Schwa says.

"Yeah," I said. "They'd dissect him and put him in a formaldehyde fish tank in Area 51."

Howie shook his head. "Area 51 is for aliens," he says. "They'd probably put him in Area 52."

"Maybe we should try something that isn't so big," I suggested. "Maybe just stuff around school. I'm sure there are people around here who would pay for the services of a Stealth Schwa." At first this had just been my lips flapping, like they often do—but every once in a while my lips flap and something brilliant flies out. I realized that maybe I was onto something here.

"How much do you think people would pay?" the Schwa asked.

I took an outside shot. "How much is the stealth fighter worth?" *Clank!* Nothing but chain. I reveled in the sound.

LAB JOURNAL
The Schwa Effect: Experiment #3

Hypothesis: The Schwa can pass through airport security with an iron bar in his pocket.

Materials: JFK American Airlines terminal, a six-inch iron bar, and the Schwa.

Procedure: The Schwa was asked to walk through the security checkpoint, go to Gate B-17, then walk back.

Results: The Schwa stood in line at the security checkpoint, but the guy who was checking IDs and airplane tickets skipped right past him. The Schwa gave us the A-okay sign. Then he walked through the metal detector, and it buzzed. Security then noticed him. They made him raise his arms, passing a wand all over him until finding the iron bar. They called more security over and two national guardsmen dressed in camouflage. They asked where his parents were and wanted to see his ticket. That's when the rest of us came forward to explain that it was just an experiment and not to get all bent out of shape. The national guardsmen and security officers weren't happy. They called our parents. They were not happy either. This ends our experimentation on the Schwa Effect.

Conclusion:

1. The Schwa is unnoticed by your generic security guard unless he's tipped off to his presence by advanced technology like a metal detector.

2. Iron bars in the Schwa's pocket are still iron bars.

Making Big Bucks off of Stealth Economics, Because Maybe I Got Some Business Sense

4 Once we decided to turn the Schwa Effect into a money-making proposition, it wasn't hard to get the ball rolling. When we had presented our series of Schwa experiments to the class, most everyone laughed, figuring it was a joke—but enough of our classmates had been part of the experiments to suspect there was something more to it. You know, it's like that TV show where the psychic dude talked to your dead relatives—all of whom seem to be just hanging around, watching everything you do . . . which is really disturbing when you stop to think about it. You don't *really* believe it, but there's enough borderline credibility to make you wonder.

That's how it was with the Schwa. It was too much for most kids to really believe the Schwa Effect, but people were curious—and curiosity was a key element of Stealth Economics. Mary Ellen MacCaw was the first to offer hard cash.

"I wanna see the Schwa do something," she said to me in the

hall after school. Most everyone else had left, so we were pretty much alone.

"Do what?" I asked.

"I don't know. Something."

"The Schwa doesn't do things for free."

Mary Ellen reached into her pocket, jangled around in there for a while, and came up with four quarters. She handed them to me.

"For a dollar, the Schwa will appear out of thin air."

"Where?" said Mary Ellen. "When?"

"Here and now," said the Schwa.

And she jumped. I've never seen anyone jump like that except while watching a horror movie—because the Schwa had been standing right next to her all along.

She bumped into a locker and the sound echoed down the hallway. "How do you *do* that?!" she asked the Schwa.

"Guess you could call it a 'hidden' talent."

As Mary Ellen's mouth was almost as big as her nose, by the next day people were waiting in line to pay the price and share in the Schwa Experience.

My dad says that at Pisher Plastics they believe anything can be marketed and sold. "They'd put a price tag on a dead rat if they thought it would sell," he once told me. "Then they'd hire an advertising firm to show beautiful women wearing them on their shoulders. It's all part of a free-market economy."

I can't vouch for the dead-rat theory, but I do know that in our local free-market economy, the Schwa was a high-ticket item—and as his manager, lining up his jobs, I got a decent percentage of the money he made. I gotta admit, though, the money was just gravy. It was great for once to be the center of attention—or at least positioned next to the center of attention. Funny how the Schwa could be right in the middle and still go unseen.

"It's a waste of time," Ira said, when I asked him if he and Howie wanted in on our business venture.

"Yeah," said Howie. "I can think of a hundred better ways to make money."

They were still pretty annoyed about the grade we had gotten on our Schwa experiments. "F for eFFort," Mr. Werthog had said. He thought the whole thing was a scam when, for once, it wasn't. After that, Ira and Howie wanted nothing to do with Stealth Economics.

"Why don't you forget this Schwa thing and help with my next movie," Ira said. *"Gerritsen Beach Beauties."*

"I'm casting director," says Howie, beaming with pride that may have just been hormones.

I told them no, because I couldn't just bail on the Schwa.

"Suit yourself," Ira said. "But when we're surrounded by babes begging for a part in the film, don't come crying to us."

In the end no girls were stupid enough to audition for them, so they had to settle for Claymation. Stealth Economics, on the other hand, turned out to be a much better business decision than anyone thought.

Once Mary Ellen MacCaw spread the word, people began to devise more and more uses for the Schwa's unique talent. A bunch of jocks paid the Schwa ten bucks to eavesdrop on a gaggle of cheerleaders and find out which guys they were talking about. I negotiated an eighteen-dollar deal for the Schwa to slip a kid's late book report into a teacher's briefcase, right beneath the teacher's nose.

"We want to put the Schwa on retainer," our eighth-grade student officers told us barely a week into our little business. In other words, they wanted to pay him a lot of money ahead of time so they could ask him to do whatever they wanted, whenever they wanted it.

"Cool," the Schwa said.

"How much?" I asked.

I negotiated them up to ten bucks a week for service-on-demand. The Schwa cost more than cable!

They used him a lot in the first few weeks he was on retainer. Mostly they asked him to go into the teachers' lounge, hang out in a corner, and report back to the student government on all gossip. He always slipped in right behind one of the fatter teachers, and never got caught. The student officers also had him hang out in the cafeteria kitchen to see who was mooching all those missing snack cakes, because the principal was blaming it on students. It turned out to be Mr. Spanks, the school security guard.

"We'd like to sign him up as an investigative reporter," the journalism class said, after they heard how old Spanky got busted. But the class officers made a big stink since they already had him on retainer, claiming we couldn't work for both government and the press, so we had to tell them no.

The jobs made us decent money for doing nothing more than not getting noticed—but it was dares that payed the most, depending on how many kids paid into it. Since I acted as the bank, paying out of my own pocket when we lost, the Schwa and I shared our dare winnings fifty-fifty.

"I dare the Schwa to walk into the principal's office, thumb his nose at Principal Assinette, then leave, without being seen."

Piece of cake. Total take: $32.

"I dare the Schwa to cut in front of Guido Buccafeo in the lunch line without being noticed, then dip his finger in Guido's mashed potatoes, and not get beaten up."

No problem. Total take: $26.

"I dare the Schwa to spend an entire day at school wearing nothing but a Speedo and not be noticed by his teachers."

We lost twenty-two bucks on that one, but he made it all the way to third period!

I told the Schwa he was like Millard Fillmore—the president famous for going unnoticed—and as his manager, I found my middle-finger syndrome fading away. I was suddenly being treated with respect.

"It's all gonna crash and burn," Ira kept telling me after Ralphy Sherman started spreading the rumor that the Schwa could teleport. No one believed it, but it still damaged our credibility. "It's like Las Vegas," Ira said. "No matter how much you *think* you're winning, the odds are stacked against you."

I reminded him we had already scientifically proven that the odds were on our side. "We can still cut you in on the action," I offered him—and then I had to add, "You can take your money and buy more clay." Ira was not amused.

Still, no matter how much he and Howie frowned on our scheme, it didn't faze the Schwa, so I tried not to let it faze me.

"You oughta go into business school, Antsy," the Schwa told me as we scarfed down fries at Fuggettaburger. "You've got a real knack for it."

"Naah," I said. "I'm just leeching off of you." But still, what he said struck a chord in me—and no minor chord either. It was the first time anyone ever accused me of having any real talent. I mean, my mother sometimes says I should go into astrophysics, but that's just because I'm good at taking up time and space.

I don't know what came over me then. Maybe I felt I knew the Schwa well enough—or maybe I was just talented at screwing up a good situation. Whatever the reason, I turned to him and asked: "So, Schwa—what really happened to your mother?"

I felt him go stiff. I mean I really felt it, like we were connected in some freaky way. He finished his fries, I finished mine. We left. Then, just as we hit the street, he said, "She disappeared when I was five." And then he added, "Don't ask me again, okay?"

As for what happened next, call it fate, call it luck, call it whatever you want, but the next dare was the one that changed our lives. It could be that both of our lives were leading up to this moment. But I always wonder what would have happened if we didn't take Wendell Tiggor's dare.

I already told you about Old Man Crawley—the hermit who lived on the second floor of his massive restaurant that took up a whole block on the bay. I think every neighborhood in the world's got a shut-in. There's all these reasons for it, y'know, like outdooraphobia, or whatever they call it. They love to make movies about shut-ins, and it always turns out that it's some lonely dude who's just misunderstood. But that wasn't the case with Charles J. Crawley. Nothing to misunderstand about him. He was old, he was rich, he was cranky, and although no one ever saw or actually spoke to him, he made it very clear he was not to be messed with.

There was this one Halloween, for instance, some of the

neighborhood kids, including my brother, went on an egg patrol—and there are lots of windows to egg on that second floor of Crawley's restaurant. We never did see Crawley himself looking out of the windows, but there were always Afghans poking their noses out. So, anyway, my brother and some of his friends, they go out on Halloween a few years back, toss a few eggs at Crawley's upstairs windows, and run off. We heard nothing about it, except for one thing . . . from November 1 until New Year's Day, not a single market in the neighborhood had eggs—not even the big supermarket chains. "It's a local shortage," people were told—but everyone knew that it was Old Man Crawley. He had pulled some strings and shut down the egg supply to the whole neighborhood. No one ever egged his windows again.

Which brings me to the biggest and potentially most profitable dare that our little invisibility enterprise with the Schwa took on. Like I said, it was Wendell Tiggor's dare. It was a pretty clever one, which makes me think he didn't actually come up with it, because Wendell Tiggor had about the intelligence of my mother's meat loaf if you took out the onions. It was at the bus stop after school that Tiggor came up to me.

"So, I've been hearing about this Schwa kid." (Tiggor begins every sentence with the word "so.")

"Yeah?"

"So, I hear he goes invisible or something."

"Why don't you ask him yourself?" I say. "He's standing right here."

"Where?"

"Right in front of your face."

"Hi," said Schwa, who happened to be next to me and, I might add, directly in Tiggor's line of sight.

"Oh." Tiggor squinted his beady eyes and looked him over. "So, he doesn't look invisible to me."

"Then why didn't you see him when you were staring straight at him?" Tiggor has to think about that one. You can almost hear rusty gears turning in his head, like one of those farm combines that sat out in the rain too long. I figured if I let those gears turn anymore, one might come flying out of his ear and kill some innocent bystander. "Never mind," I say. "What can we do for you?" By now a few other kids have started to take notice of our conversation.

"So, I hear you do stuff," he says to the Schwa.

"Talk to my manager," says the Schwa. Tiggor's lip curls in confusion.

"He means me. Is it a service you wish my client to provide? Because if it's a service, you'll have to clear it with the student officers, who have him on retainer. Government regulations. You know how it is. Of course if it's a dare instead of a service, we can do that, no problem." At the word "dare," even more kids moved into listening range. Six or seven were clustered around us, and as everyone knows, when there's a few kids in a group it draws more and more, like curiosity has its own gravity.

"It's a dare," says Tiggor.

"Dares come with a price, too; what do you want the Schwa to do?"

"You say he can do things and not be seen," Tigger says. "So let's see if he can go into Old Man Crawley's and bring something back." A bus came and went, but none of the kids got on. The public buses run every ten minutes, and this was worth ten minutes of everyone's time.

"Let me consult with my client."

I pull the Schwa aside, and he whispers, "I don't know, Antsy."

Tiggor laughs. "See, I told you," he says to the other kids. "He's a fake. Ain't no such thing as an invisible boy."

"Well, he *did* walk through the girls' locker room without getting seen," one kid says.

"So," says Tiggor, "does he have the pictures to prove it?"

"Yeah," I tell Tiggor, "you *wish* you had pictures."

Tiggor looks at me and hooks his thumbs in his pockets like he's a gunslinger ready to draw. "Twenty bucks says he can't do it."

"You're on," I said without a second thought—such is my faith in the Schwa. But the Schwa tugs my sleeve.

"Antsy . . ."

"What do you want him to bring back?"

"So, how about a dog bowl," Tiggor says. Everybody agrees that's the perfect item. There's about twenty kids around us now.

"Anybody else care to take the wager?" I ask.

The kids who had seen the Schwa in action all looked down and shook their heads. Only those who were not yet believers would bet against the Schwa.

"I'm in for five bucks," says one kid.

"Two bucks over here," says another. And by the time the betting frenzy's over, fifty-four bucks are on the line.

We caught the next bus, and all the way home the Schwa was bouncing his knees up and down like he's gotta go pee, but I know it's because he's all nervous.

"Come on, Schwa, take it easy. There are so many dogs in there, you'll probably trip on a bowl on the way in."

"And if I get caught?"

"If you get caught, I pay everyone fifty-four bucks out of my own pocket—no loss to you, except maybe loss of life—but that's a real long shot." I was only kidding, but he took it seriously. I began to feel a bit lousy for rushing into the dare without checking out his feelings first.

"We can always back out," I told him.

He didn't like the sound of that either—it would make him look chicken. "It's just that everyone's heard how creepy Old Man Crawley is. There are all these rumors about him."

"So? There are rumors about you, too."

"Yeah," said the Schwa. "And some of them are true."

He had me there, although I didn't have the nerve to ask which ones. "Listen; if you actually go in there, you'll be going in as just some guy—but you'll be coming out as a legend: the one kid ever to penetrate Brooklyn's last great mystery."

That hooked him. "People remember legends, don't they?"

"Always."

The Schwa nodded. "Okay, then. I'm gonna nab myself a dog bowl."

Which Is Worse: Getting Mauled by a Pack of Dogs, or Getting Your Brains Bashed Out by a Steel Poker?

5 We set the operation for Sunday morning, 10 A.M. Wendell Tiggor and a cluster of Tiggorhoids showed up to witness and make sure we didn't just go out and buy a dog dish somewhere, then say we got it from Crawley's. A bunch of the other kids who had bet against us were there, too, leaning against a railing across the street, so when the Schwa and I ride up on our bikes there are all these kids already there, looking way too suspicious. It's called loitering, which is like littering with human beings as the trash. I checked to see if Crawley's looking out on us, but all I see in the dark windows above the restaurant are a couple of furry dog faces in front of closed curtains.

"So we thought you'd chickened out," Tiggor says.

The Schwa took off his jacket. He was strategically dressed in dark brown; the same color as Crawley's curtains. He walked over to the railing that overlooked the murky water of the bay, and stretched like this was an Olympic event.

At this point I was beginning to get nervous for him. "Listen," I say, "you might go unnoticed around people, but I don't know about dogs. Our experiments didn't include dogs. What if you're like one of those whistles that people can't hear, but dogs can—or what if they can smell you? We don't know if you got a stealthy odor."

He sniffed his armpit, then looked at me. "I smell stealthy to me. Want a whiff?"

"I'll pass."

"So what's taking so long?" says Tiggor. "Are you gonna do it or not, because I ain't got all day."

"Hey, this is a delicate procedure," I tell him. "The Schwa's gotta get himself mentally prepared."

Tiggor gave an apelike grunt. I took the Schwa aside. "Just remember, I'll be right outside. If you need help, you signal to me and I'll be there in a second."

"I know you will, Antsy. Thanks."

I swear, it felt like he was going off to war and not into some cranky old geezer's place. The thing is, none of the other dares had the Schwa venturing into the unknown, unless you count the locker room. Crawley, even without ever being seen, was scary—and who knew if any of those Afghans were trained to kill.

I went around back with him, where a fire-escape ladder led up to the building's second story. Old Man Crawley's apartment was huge, filling the whole second floor—the only way in was through the restaurant itself—but by looking down from the roof of an apartment building a few blocks away, we had learned that there was a little courtyard patio in the middle of his apartment, open to the sky. That would be our point of entry.

The stench of yesterday's lobster wafted out of the Dumpster behind the restaurant, smelling like a fish market on a hot day, or my aunt Mona (trust me, you don't wanna know). Ignoring the smell, we hopped up to the lip of the Dumpster so we could reach the fire-escape ladder. I gently pulled it down, trying to keep it from squeaking. The Schwa climbed on.

"Stealth is wealth," I said to him, which has been our little good-luck phrase ever since we started taking dares.

"Stealth is wealth," he said back. We punched knuckles, and he climbed up, disappearing onto the roof. I crossed the street and waited at the edge of the bay with the others.

Tiggor looked at the windows of Crawley's place, then looked at me. "So what do we do now?"

I shrugged. "We wait."

Turns out we didn't have to wait long. Although I wasn't there to see what happened, it probably went something like this:

The Schwa jumps down into the little enclosed patio filled with gravel, and more dog crap than you ever want to see in one place. A door is ajar so the dogs can come and go from the patio as they please. This is the door the Schwa slips into.

The place is dark. The lightbulbs are just twenty-five watts behind dark lamp shades, and no sunlight makes it through those thick curtains. The Schwa stands there in the living room, waiting for his eyes to adjust to the dim light. There are two dogs fighting over a piece of knotted rope across the room. They don't notice him. He does have a stealthy odor! Or the dogs are just too old to smell. He hears a TV on in another room somewhere far away in the huge apartment.

So where are the dog bowls?

He makes his way through the living room, across a formal dining room with a long table that hasn't seen a dinner party in a millennium, and then he strikes gold. Fourteen dog bowls are lined up nice and neat against a kitchen wall. Products of Pisher Plastics.

All he has to do is take one of the bowls and get out the way he came. That's all.

He bends down, grabs a bowl, and then he discovers something awful: All fourteen bowls are nailed to the ground.

And now he begins to think that maybe he's like a dog whistle after all, because there's an Afghan growling in his face . . .

Meanwhile, from outside, I saw all the dogs suddenly disappear from the windows. This was not a good sign. I heard all this barking, then a man yelling, although it was too muffled to hear what he yelled.

And Wendell Tiggor laughs. "So you lose," he says. "Pay up."

In the window I now saw the Schwa pressed up against the glass, hiding behind the curtains. I knew he couldn't last like that for long.

"Think the dogs'll eat him?" says one of the other kids.

I didn't have time for idiots. Instead I took off across the street, toward the building, nearly becoming roadkill because I didn't look both ways like every kid's mother told them from the beginning of time. Narrowly surviving the busy avenue, I made it around back to the fire escape. I didn't know what to do, but I couldn't just leave the Schwa stranded like that. *Leave no man behind*—isn't that what they say in battle?

I scrambled to the roof, leaped into the little patio, and burst through the open door.

In a second the dogs were barreling toward me. I tensed up,

preparing to get bit. The dogs advanced, held their ground, and then backed away, not sure whether to protect their master, their home, or themselves. The smell of dog was everywhere. Dog food, dog fur, dog breath. The smell was overpowering, and the barking endless and loud. I didn't dare move—but I glanced to the curtains where I knew the Schwa was hiding. Any dogs that had been sniffing around there had come over toward me. With any luck, the Schwa would be able to slip out unnoticed. As for me, well, I suppose this was what I have to do to earn my 50 percent. Damage control.

"Get out of here!" said a voice much fuller, much stronger than I expected.

My eyes still hadn't adjusted to the dim light, so I wasn't sure what I was seeing at first. A low square shape moved at me through a doorway. Only when it pushed through the dogs could I see what it was. It was a wheelchair. Old Man Crawley was in a wheelchair.

"Don't move a muscle, or I'll have them tear you to shreds, if I don't do it myself."

He held a fireplace poker in the air as he rolled the chair forward with his other hand. His hair was gray and slicked back. His jaw was hard and square—it looked like he still had all his teeth, which is more than I can say for my own relatives that age. He wore a white shirt buttoned all the way to the neck, where loose skin flopped around like on a turkey—but mostly it was the poker that held my attention. The thing looked heavy, the thing looked sharp, and people in wheelchairs usually have lots of upper-body strength.

"Which do you want?" I said.

"What?"

"You said 'get out of here,' and 'don't move a muscle.' I can't do both."

"You're a wiseass."

Not at all happy with their master's tone of voice, the dogs were now baring their teeth at me, in addition to barking and growling.

"I can explain," I said, which I really couldn't, but don't you always say that when you get caught doing something you shouldn't be doing?

"I have already called the police. They will be here momentarily to arrest you, at which time you will be prosecuted to the fullest extent of the law."

Which was good, because it meant he didn't plan to kill me with the poker, or with the dogs. "Please, Mr. Crawley, I didn't mean anything. It was just a bet, see? On a dare to get a dog bowl. That's all. I would have given it back. I swear."

"The dog bowls are nailed down," he informed me.

"My mistake."

"How much did you bet?"

"Fifty-four dollars," I told him.

"You just lost fifty-four dollars."

"Yeah, I guess so. So can I go now? It's punishment enough, right?"

"Fifty-four dollars is hardly a sufficient fine for breaking and entering, attempted theft, and the assault of an elderly man—"

"But . . . wait . . . I didn't assault you!"

He smiled viciously. "Who do you think the police will believe, me or you?"

By now most of the dogs had quieted down. A few had wandered off, a couple came over to sniff at me, but the rest all clustered protectively around the old man.

"I really am sorry, Mr. Crawley."

"There are countries where delinquent children are caned for their misdeeds. Do you know what caning is?"

"Kind of like whipping?"

"Yes," he said, "but more painful. You'd probably choose a few dog bites over a caning."

He put the poker down across the arms of his wheelchair. "You can tell your friend to come out from behind the curtains now."

My heart sank. "What friend?"

"Lying does not help your case," snapped Crawley.

Before I could say any more, the Schwa emerged from behind the curtains, looking sheepish, like a dog who just dirtied the rug.

"How did you know he was there?"

"Let's just say I'm observant," said Crawley. "I don't usually keep sneakers poking out from beneath my curtains."

Four out of five people didn't notice the Schwa. It figures Crawley had to be a fifth person. He stared at us there, saying nothing, waiting for the police to arrive.

"I . . . I didn't know you were an invalid," I said, which is a pretty stupid thing to say, but my brain tends to become spongelike when under stress.

Crawley frowned. I thought he already *was* frowning. "I broke a hip," he said, annoyed. "The wheelchair is only temporary."

"Sorry."

"Sorry sorry sorry," he mocked. "You sound like a broken record."

"Sorry," I said, then grimaced.

"What's your name?"

"Wendell Tiggor," I said, without missing a beat.

"Very good. Now tell me your real name."

This guy might have been old, but he was as sharp as a shark tooth. I sighed. "Anthony Bonano."

He turned to the Schwa. "And your name?"

I had hoped he might have forgotten the Schwa was there, but luck was in short supply today.

"Calvin. Calvin Schwa."

"Stupid name."

"I know, sir. It wasn't my choice, sir."

I could hear sirens now, getting closer. I supposed Wendell and the Tiggorhoids had all deserted. No one in that crowd would risk their necks, or any other part of their anatomy, for us.

"Well, there they are," said Crawley, hearing the sirens. "Tell me, is this your first arrest, or are you repeat offenders?"

As we weren't actually arrested at the American Airlines terminal, I told him it was a first offense.

"It won't be the last, I'm sure," he said.

I cleared my throat. "Excuse me, sir, but I think it will be."

"Will be what?"

"I think it will be the last time I'm arrested."

"I find that hard to believe." He leaned over, scratching one of his dogs behind the ears. "Can't change breeding, isn't that right, Avarice?"

The dog purred.

Breeding? Now I was getting mad. "My breeding is fine," I told him. The Schwa, who's still mostly petrified, hits me to shut me up, but I don't. "If you ask me, it's *your* breeding that's all screwed up."

Crawley raised his eyebrows and gripped his poker. "Is that so."

"It must take some pretty bad genes to turn someone into a miserable old man who'd send a couple of kids to jail just for trying to get a plastic dog bowl."

He scowled at me for a long time. The sound of sirens peaked, then stopped right outside. Then he said, "Genes aren't everything. You failed to take environment into account."

"Well, so did you."

There came an urgent knocking at the door, and all the dogs went running toward it, barking. "Mr. Crawley," said a muffled voice through the door, over the chorus of barks. "Mr. Crawley, are you all right?"

The old man gave the Schwa and me a twisted grin. "Destiny calls." He rolled off toward the door, calling back to us, "Either of you try to escape and I'll have you shot."

I didn't really believe that, but I also didn't want to take any chances.

"This is bad, Antsy," the Schwa said. "Real bad."

"Tell me something I don't know."

Crawley rolled back in about a minute. Amazingly, no police officers were with him. "I told them it was a false alarm."

The sigh of relief rolled off the Schwa and me like a wave. "Thank you, Mr. Crawley."

He ignored us. "The police will only give you a slap on the wrist, and since you're not crying hysterically in terror right now, I assume your parents will not beat you. Therefore I will administer your punishment personally. You will return here tomorrow by the *front* door, at three o'clock sharp, and begin working off your transgression. If you fail to come, I will find out what your parents do for a living, and I will have them fired."

"You can't do that!"

"I've found I can do anything I please."

I thought it was just an idle threat, but then I remembered the great egg shortage. A man like Crawley had more money than God in a good economy, as my father would say, and probably had friends in both high and low places. If he said he'd have my father fired, I figured I should believe it.

"What will you pay us?" I asked.

"Nothing."

"That's slavery!"

"No," said Crawley, with a grin so wide it stretched his wrinkles straight. "*That's* community service."

As If I Didn't Already Have Enough Annoying Things to Do Every Day, Now I Gotta Do This

6 I wasn't too hungry at dinner that night. Sure, I was no stranger to failed schemes, but never had one backfired so badly. The fifty-four bucks were the least of my worries, now that Crawley was pulling our strings. It was enough to kill any appetite.

For the entire meal I just sort of moved my food around my plate. My parents didn't notice, mainly because I wasn't Frankie or Christina. If Christina doesn't eat, right away they're feeling her forehead to see if she's got a fever. As for Frankie, not eating isn't one of his problems. He's more likely to get yelled at for taking all the food. Once I tried to take a huge plateful like Frankie does, just to see what my parents would do. While I wasn't looking, Frankie moved some food from my plate to his, and my parents got on his case instead of mine. He always complains that I get away with everything. Well, there are two sides to that wooden nickel.

I was unnaturally quiet for most of the meal, which was

probably a mistake, because it threw off the entire family equilibrium.

Mom and Dad had begun a conversation about what sort of carpeting to put down in our unfinished finished basement. You have to understand that my parents live to bicker. You could stick them at the beach and they'd argue whether the ocean was bluish green, or greenish blue.

They rarely argued over dinner, though, I think because when you eat, your blood rushes from your brain to your stomach, putting you at a strategic disadvantage, because how are you going to come up with the real zingers when your brain isn't at full power?

Like I said, it started as a discussion, and then it began heating up to the point where I would usually throw in some wisecrack. When I didn't, the discussion suddenly evolved into an argument.

"We already agreed it should be Berber!" Mom says.

"I never agreed to anything! The carpet in the basement should match the rest of the house." It's escalating to the point where food is flying out of their mouths while they talk. Frankie just shakes his head, Christina's reaching for her journal, and I start thinking about dog collars, maybe because dogs are on my mind after being at Crawley's. When dogs bark too much, you can put on special collars, so each time the dog barks, it squirts out a funky smell. It doesn't really teach dogs not to bark, but it distracts them long enough to make 'em forget they were barking.

I decided to let the carpet argument build just a bit more, then dropped my fork on my plate loudly. "Jeez! What's the big deal? Put down a hardwood floor and each of you can buy a rug."

"Watch that fork, you'll break the plate!" Mom says.

"What? Are *you* gonna pay for a wood floor?" Dad grumbles.

"My friend's got a wood closet to keep away bugs," says Christina.

"That's cedar," Mom explains.

"We oughta build a cedar closet," says Dad.

And that was that. The conversation lapsed into an endless stream of other topics, and I went back to pushing my food around my plate. They never noticed I had stopped the argument, just like they didn't notice I wasn't eating. Sometimes the Schwa had nothing on me.

"What do you think he'll make us do?" the Schwa asked as we walked as slow as we dared from school to Crawley's the next afternoon.

"I really don't want to think about it." Truth was, I spent most of the night thinking about it. I could barely get my homework done, which is not all that unusual, but this time it wasn't because of TV, or video games, or my friends. It was because all I could think of were the many forms of torture Crawley could devise. I once had a teacher who said my imagination was about as developed as my appendix, but I don't agree, because I came up with a whole bunch of possibilities of what Crawley could do. He could make us clean his dog-fouled patio with our toothbrushes—they do stuff like that in the army, I hear. He could send us on dangerous errands to Mafia types where we might get whacked, because anyone *that* rich in Brooklyn has gotta know a few of those guys. Or what if he wanted us to move the bodies he's got locked up in a cellar beneath the restaurant? At three in the morning, when you're tossing in bed, it sounds almost possible, proving that my imagination is alive and well, or, I guess I should say, alive and sick.

"I think we're gonna wish we were arrested," I told the Schwa.

The restaurant only had a few customers at this hour of the afternoon. We identified ourselves to the maître d', who I guess doubled as Crawley's doorman for what few visitors he got.

"Ah," said the maître d'oorman, "Mr. Crawley is expecting you. Follow me."

He glided up the grand staircase real smooth, like it was a fast escalator and not stairs, then he took us through an unused part of the restaurant stacked with dusty old tables and broken chairs. We went down a hallway that led to the door of Mr. Crawley's private residence.

"Mr. Crawley, those boys are here," the maître d'oorman said as he knocked. Barking and the pounding of paws followed. Then I could hear all the bolts sliding open on the other side, and Crawley pulled open the door while blocking the escape of the dogs with his wheelchair.

"You're five minutes early," he said, the tone in his voice like we were half an hour late.

We stepped in, he pushed the door closed behind us, a dog yelped because his nose got caught in the door for an instant, and there we were.

Crawley reached into the pocket of his fancy robe—a dinner jacket, I think it's called. The kind of thing Professor Plum would wear before killing Colonel Mustard in the ballroom with the candlestick. From the pocket he pulled a few doggie treats and hurled them over his shoulder so the dogs would leave us alone.

"I've decided to sentence the two of you to twelve weeks of community service," he said. "Mr. Bonano, from this day forward, you shall be responsible for the sins. You, Mr. Schwa, shall be responsible for the virtues. Take all the time you need each day, but by no means are you to complete the task any earlier than five P.M. Now get to it."

I looked at the Schwa, the Schwa looked at me. I felt like I had just been called up to the board to explain an Einstein theory, but I don't think Einstein could figure this one out, even if he was alive.

"Why are you staring like imbeciles? Didn't you hear me?"

"Yeah, we heard you," I said. "Sins and virtues. Now would you mind speaking in English that people who aren't, like, ninety years old can understand?"

He scowled at us. He was really good at that. Then he spoke, very slowly, as if to morons. "The seven virtues, and the seven deadly sins. *Comprendo?*"

"*Oigo,*" I said, *"pero no comprendo."* I hear, but I don't understand. At last my two years of Spanish had paid off! It was worth it for the surprised look on Crawley's face—to see that, as Howie would put it, I was only half the moron he thought I was.

"Great," mumbled the Schwa. "Now he's really gonna be pissed off."

But instead of saying anything, Crawley put two fingers in his mouth and whistled. All the dogs came running.

As they crowded around him, jockeying for position, he touched each of them on the head and announced: "Prudence, Temperance, Justice, Fortitude, Faith, Hope, and Charity." He took a breath, then continued: "Envy, Sloth, Anger, Lust,

Gluttony, Pride, and Avarice. Do you understand now, or shall I get you a translator?"

"You want each of us to walk seven dogs each, every day."

"Gold star for you."

Crawley peered at me, but I just returned his unpleasant gaze. "Why not Greed?" I said.

"Excuse me?"

"Avarice is Greed, right? That's the way I learned the seven deadly sins. So why not just name the dog Greed?"

"Don't you know anything?" Crawley growled. "Avarice is a much better name for a dog."

He spun his wheelchair and rolled into the deeper recesses of his apartment. "Leashes are hanging in the kitchen." And he was gone.

At first we tried to walk them two at a time, but they were so strong, so untrained, and so excited to be outside, they practically pulled us into oncoming traffic. There were no shortcuts. We each could only handle one dog at a time. Walking dogs for no pay for two hours a day wasn't exactly my idea of fun. But the Schwa and I did it. We could have gotten out of it. We could have just told our parents what we had done, and taken whatever punishment they dealt out. Even if Crawley went to the police, they wouldn't do much about it—especially after we had shown what decent guys we were by volunteering to walk his dogs for those first few days. Still, we kept on doing it. Maybe it's because there was a kind of a mystique to it, walking the infamous Old Man Crawley's dogs. Everyone knew whose dogs they were—it's not like the neighborhood is teeming with

Afghans. Somehow it made us important. Or maybe we kept on doing it because we gave him our word. I can't speak for the Schwa, but for me, my word had never really meant much of anything. I can't count all the times I gave someone my word, then flaked out. This time was different, though, because if I didn't keep my word, Crawley would be able to sit in his dark apartment and gloat. He'd see it as proof that I was at the shallow end of the gene pool, and I wouldn't give him that satisfaction, no matter how many barking sins I had to walk.

"Hey, Bonano," said Wendell Tiggor from across the street while we walked Charity and Gluttony that first week. "So I like your new girlfriend," he says, pointing to the dog. "She's got real animal attraction."

"We'd let you have one," I told him, "but we don't got one called Stupidity." The Schwa and I high-fived as best we could with two dogs pulling us down the street.

Walking dogs also meant there was less time to hang out with my other friends. Namely, Howie and Ira. It's not like they made any extra effort to see me anyway.

During our second week of canine slavery, however, Howie *did* join the Schwa and me for a few minutes one afternoon while we walked Hope and Lust.

"I can't hang out long," says Howie. "I gotta walk my little brother to tae kwan do."

"Is he a sin or a virtue?" the Schwa asked, but it goes right over Howie's head.

I thought he might offer to help us walk the dogs, at least for a minute, but his hands stayed firmly shoved in his pockets. "Is Crawley as crazy as they say?"

I tugged on the leash to keep Lust from going after a passing poodle. "Well, let's put it this way: If he's got bats in his belfry, he nails them to the wall to watch them wriggle."

The Schwa laughed.

"He's real mean, huh?" says Howie.

"He hates the world and the world hates him right back." What I didn't say was how much the nasty old guy was growing on me. I actually looked forward to seeing him, just so I could irritate him.

Right about now Howie looks over his shoulder like the FBI might be reporting his activities to his parents, who have recently begun a policy of preemptive grounding. "Listen, I gotta go. So long, Antsy," and he takes off.

It would have been all fine and good, except for one thing. He didn't say good-bye to the Schwa. It seemed to slip his mind that the Schwa was even there. I could tell the Schwa didn't like this, but he didn't say anything about it—he just looked down at Hope, who was happily sniffing gum spots on the sidewalk.

We were heading back to Crawley's for the next two dogs when the Schwa broke the silence. "They didn't even notice it was orange?" he said.

"What?"

"The sombrero. Not a single person noticed it was orange? Not a single person even noticed it was a *sombrero?*"

It was the first time he had mentioned the experiments. When we were doing them, he seemed fine. He took a scientific interest in the results. It had never occurred to me that they might have bothered him.

"Not one."

"Hmm," he said, shaking his head. "Go figure."

"Hey, it's not a bad thing," I told him. "This Schwa Effect. It's a natural ability—you know, like those people who can memorize the phone book and stuff—'idiot savants.'" This was just getting worse by the minute. "Anyway, it's a skill you oughta be proud of."

"Yeah? Well, tell me how proud you feel when you don't get a report card because the teacher forgot to make you one. Or when the bus doesn't stop for you because the driver doesn't notice you're at the stop. Or when your own father makes dinner for himself but not for you because it slipped his mind that you were there."

"You're making that up," I finally said. "That doesn't happen."

"Oh yeah? Come to my house for dinner sometime."

The Schwa hadn't really meant it as an invitation, but I took it as one. I was curious. I had to know just what kind of home environment could turn out an invisible-ish kid. That, and I wanted to know more about his mysteriously missing mother, but I didn't dare tell him that. I figured his reluctance to talk about his home life must have been because he was embarrassed about it—like maybe he lived in a broken-down shack, or something.

The Schwa lived at the edge of our neighborhood, on a street I never had been on before. When I arrived there, I have to say I was disappointed by what I saw. It was a row of small two-story homes, packed in tight, with driveways in between. His house wasn't invisible. It wasn't even unnoticeable. In fact, it stood out. All the other homes on the street had fake plastic siding. You know the stuff—plastic that's supposed to look like aluminum that's supposed to look like wood. While the rest of the homes were white, eggshell, or light blue, the Schwa's house was canary yellow. I had to double-check the address to make sure I had the right place. The front yard was well cared for. There was even a little bubbling rock fountain in the corner that appeared to actually be made of rock and not Pisher Plastic. It was *exemplary,* to borrow a word I missed on my last vocabulary test: the perfect example of what a front yard should be.

There was a doormat that said: IF YOU LIVED HERE, YOU'D BE HOME RIGHT NOW, AND I'D HAVE NO MORTGAGE. I could hear music playing somewhere inside. Guitar. I rang the bell, and in a moment the door opened and no one appeared to be standing there.

"Hi, Schwa."

"Hi, Antsy." The shadows fell just the right way to camouflage him against the rest of the room. I blinked a few times, and he came into focus. He didn't sound particularly pleased that I was there. It was more like he was resigned to the fact. He showed me in and introduced me to his father.

They say the apple doesn't fall far from the tree, but looking at the Schwa and his father, I would say the apple rolled clear into an orange grove. The man was about as un-Schwa-like as could be. He wore white overalls with paint stains all over them—the Schwa had said he was a housepainter. Right now he wasn't painting, he was sitting in the living room playing a twelve-string guitar—I mean *really* playing, not just strumming. He had a ponytail with a few strands of gray, the same color as his guitar strings.

Not only was he visible, but he actually stood out.

"Are you sure you're not adopted?" I asked. But I could tell there was enough of a resemblance to make DNA testing un-necessary.

"I look like him," Schwa said, "but in most other ways I take after my mother."

At the mention of his mother, I casually looked around for any sign of her, but there were no pictures, no feminine touches.

"Hey, Dad, this is my friend Antsy."

Mr. Schwa continued to play, not noticing.

"Dad," said the Schwa, a bit louder this time. Still he just played his guitar. The Schwa sighed.

"Mr. Schwa?" I said.

He stopped playing immediately and looked around, a bit bewildered. "Oh—you must be Calvin's friend," he said. "I'll go get him."

"I'm right here, Dad."

"Did you offer your friend something to drink?"

"You want something to drink?" the Schwa asked.

"No."

"He says no."

"Is your friend staying for dinner?"

"Yeah," I said, then whispered to the Schwa, "I thought you told him I was coming."

"I did," said the Schwa. "Twice."

It turns out the Schwa's father was terminally absentminded. There were little notes everywhere to remind him of things. The refrigerator was so full of yellow Post-it notes, it looked like Big Bird. The notes were all written by the Schwa. *Half day at school on Wednesday,* one said. *Back-to-School night on Friday,* said another. FRIEND COMING OVER FOR DINNER TONIGHT, said one in big bold letters.

"Was he always like that, or was it, like, from breathing paint fumes?" I asked after Mr. Schwa went back to playing guitar.

"He fell off a ladder a few years ago, and suffered head trauma. He's okay now, but he's like a little kid in some ways."

"Wow," I said. "So who takes care of who?"

"Exactly," says the Schwa. "But it's not so bad. And my aunt Peggy comes over a few times a week to help out."

Apparently this wasn't one of Aunt Peggy's nights. There was a raw chicken in a big pan on top of the oven. I poked the chicken. It was room temperature. Who knew how long it had been sitting out.

"Maybe we should call in for pizza."

"Naah," said the Schwa, turning on the oven to preheat. "Cooking it should kill any deadly bacteria."

The Schwa took me on the grand tour. The walls of the house were white, except one wall in each room was painted a different color. The effect was actually pretty cool. There was one forest green wall in the living room, a red wall in the kitchen, a blue wall in the dining room. The colored wall in the Schwa's room was beige. I wasn't surprised.

"So," I asked about as delicately as I could, "how long have you and your father been . . . on your own?"

"Since I was five," he said. "You wanna see my paper-clip collection?"

I replayed in my mind what he had said, certain I had somehow heard it wrong. "You're . . . kidding me, right?"

Then he reached under his bed and pulled out a box. Inside were little plastic zipper bags—at least a hundred of them—and in each one there was . . . yes, you guessed it, a paper clip.

Little ones, big ones, those fat black ones that hold whole stacks of paper together.

"Pretty cool, huh?"

I just stared, dumbfounded. "Exactly when did they release you from the nuthouse, Schwa?"

He reached into the box and pulled out a little baggie that held a silver clip. "This clip held together pages of the Nuclear Arms Treaty signed by Reagan and Gorbachev."

"No way."

I looked at it closely. It looked just like an ordinary paper clip.

He pulled out another one. It was tarnished bronze. "This one held together the original lyric sheets of 'Hey Jude.'" He pulled out another one with a blue plastic coating. "This one was clipped to a mission manual for the space shuttle."

"You mean it's been in space?"

The Schwa nodded.

"Wow!"

He showed me clip after clip, each one more exciting than the last. "Where did you get them?"

"I wrote to famous people, asking them for a paper clip from something important. You'd be amazed how many of them wrote back."

It was genius! Most of the time people are looking for the letters and documents and people that make history, but no one thinks about the little things that hold history together. Leave it to the Schwa to think of such a thing. It was, at the same time, the dullest and most interesting collection I had ever seen in my life.

Dinner wasn't ready until after nine, and it was the second

worst chicken I'd ever tasted, beaten only by a dish at a friend's birthday party that tasted more like it was made from the piñata. Even so, I was glad I had dinner with the Schwa and his father, who continued to play guitar during the meal, greasy chicken fingers and all.

"It's like he doesn't have a care in the world," I commented to the Schwa while his dad did the dishes.

"Yeah, brain damage'll do that to you," the Schwa said as he went to rewash the dishes his father didn't quite get clean. "But I wouldn't advise it."

The next night I ended up alone with my own father for dinner. Mom was off shopping with Christina, and Frankie was off with his friends, doing whatever it was honor students did on their higher plane of existence. I couldn't help but think about the Schwa, and how he came home every day to a father who might or might not feed him. That wasn't my dad. I might go unnoticed, but never unfed. And I never had to be the one taking care of him.

Dad secretly loved when Mom wasn't around for dinner, because he got the kitchen all to himself—and although none of us kids would admit it out loud, Dad was the better cook. Tonight Dad whipped up Fettucine al Bonano—his own special dish that magically transformed whatever leftovers were in the fridge into a killer pasta dish. The problem today wasn't in the cooking, it was in the eating. Dad and I never have problems talking to each other when there are other people around, but when it's just the two of us, it's like we're together on a stage and we've forgotten our lines.

"Did you break Manny yet?" he asked after a few silent minutes into the meal.

I shrugged, fettucine dangling down to my chin. "I'm not sure. His body survived detonation, but his head is missing. It could be in orbit for all we know."

"If he really turns out to be unbreakable, your old man gets a raise and a promotion."

I nodded and sucked in some more fettucine. The silence returned. I like being with my dad, but sitting across from him with nothing but food between us makes me uncomfortable. I guess I'm so used to being semivisible at home I don't know how to handle being the only available focus of attention. And now as I sat with Dad, avoiding eye contact, it hit me that maybe he felt the same way.

"They won't do both," I told him.

"What?"

"They give you a promotion so they don't have to give you a raise. They give you a raise just so they don't have to give you a promotion. They don't do both."

He looked at me, grinning and nodding like I just quoted Shakespeare. "You're right," he said. "How do you know that?"

I shrugged and thought about what the Schwa had once said about me having business savvy. "I don't know. It just makes sense." And then I added, "I probably heard it on TV or something."

We chowed down more food, barely looking at each other.

"Mom tells me you're walking dogs for that old guy who owns Crawley's."

"Yeah," I told him. "I'm being a good Philistine."

"Samaritan," he said. "I didn't even know you liked dogs."

"Neither did I."

I toyed with telling him about Old Man Crawley's threat to get him fired if I didn't walk the dogs . . . but didn't. Crawley and his dogs were my problem.

I finished up my fettucine and began thinking about what the Schwa's dinner was like tonight. Did he have to cook it himself? Did he cook for himself and his dad? Or was this one of the lucky nights when the Schwa could relax and Aunt Peggy did the cooking? Then I wondered if Aunt Peggy ever forgot to set a plate for him, like his dad.

"Listen, I was thinking about having a friend over for dinner."

"Someone new, or the usual suspects?"

"New."

"Girlfriend?"

"No such luck."

"Who?"

"They call him the Schwa."

My dad piled some more fettucine onto his plate. "What's wrong with him?"

"Does something have to be wrong with him for him to be my friend? Is that what you mean?"

"Take it easy. I just thought I heard something funny in your voice."

I didn't think my dad had it in him to tune into someone's tone. He never seemed to be able to tell when Mom was about to get mad at him, and he usually needed one of us kids to tell him what brainless, insensitive thing he had done. But this time he called it right.

I decided to be direct. "He's invisible," I said.

To my dad's credit, he took this in stride, although he did

stop chewing for a few seconds. "Does he become visible again when he takes off his ring?" Dad asked. "Does he hang out with elves and dwarfs?"

It took me a few seconds, then I got it, and laughed. "Yeah," I said. "He's got hairy feet, too."

"Well, make sure he wipes them on the doormat, or your mother will brain him."

The Lowest-Paid Male Escort
on the Entire Eastern Seaboard,
Except for Maybe the Bronx

7 Life is like a bad haircut. At first it looks awful, then you kind of get used to it, and before you know it, it grows out and you gotta get another haircut that maybe won't be so bad, unless of course you keep going to SuperClips, where the hairstylists are so terrible they oughta be using safety scissors, and when they're done you look like your head got caught in a ceiling fan. So life goes on, good haircut, bad haircut, until finally you go bald, and it don't matter no more.

I told this wisdom to my mother, and she said I oughta put it in a book, then burn it. Some people just can't appreciate the profound.

Anyway, the deal with Crawley and his dogs was like a bad haircut I was beginning to get used to. I wasn't expecting to get clipped again by a hit-and-run barber.

———

"Let Mr. Schwa go ahead. I want to talk to you alone."

Crawley always called us "Mr. Schwa" and "Mr. Bonano." At first it annoyed me on account of my teachers call us "Mr." when they were mad at us. But then, since Crawley was always mad at us, it kind of had some logic to it.

This was the third week of our dog days. Until now, Crawley had little to say to us except to comment on our unacceptable wardrobe, how unpleasant my acne was, and couldn't we find some better deodorant, because according to him, after a day of school we smelled worse than fourteen dogs. It was always an adventure with him, never knowing what he was going to gripe about when we showed up. He was usually much more on my case than the Schwa's. I assumed it was just the Schwa Effect at work. Little did I know he was sizing me up for a higher position in the Crawley Universe.

"Mr. Schwa, I said you could go."

The Schwa looked at me and shrugged. "Fine. I'll notify your next of kin, Antsy."

"Yeah, I appreciate it. If I live, I'll call you."

Once the Schwa was gone, Crawley stared at me from his wheelchair across the room for way too long.

"So what's up, Chuckles?" I had stopped calling him "sir" or Mr. Crawley. The way I figured it, those were terms of respect, and he really hadn't earned mine. Chuckles was my little nickname for him. It started as Chuck, but Chuckles seemed so much more appropriate—especially because of the way he frowned when I said it.

"I am not a clown," he said. "Kindly refrain from calling me that."

I just grinned. He frowned some more. "From now on, Mr. Schwa will walk the dogs alone."

"That's not fair," I told him. "It'll take him till nighttime."

"I will pay him," Crawley said. "Ten cents per dog per day."

"Twenty-five."

"What are you, his attorney?"

"His manager."

"I see. All right. Twenty-five."

"And that's only if he agrees."

Crawley didn't answer that—maybe because it was a fact of life that no one ever disagreed with him. "As for you, I have another task for you."

"Do I get paid, too?"

"Yes," he said without hesitation. This scared me, because Crawley gave money like bulls gave milk: not at all, and you got gored for asking. If he had already decided this was a paying job, it must be horrible beyond words.

"Your salary will depend on how well you perform your duties."

"What's the job?"

Sloth came sniffing at Crawley's pocket for treats, and the old man pushed him away. "My granddaughter will be spending the next few months with me. You will spend time with her. You will entertain her. You will pretend to like her."

I was sensing this haircut was going to be one nasty Mohawk. "What's wrong with her?"

"Why does something have to be wrong with her?" he snapped.

"I don't know," I said. "Something in your tone of voice."

Crawley wheeled himself around, banging his knee on a little end table. I knew it must have hurt, but he refused to give me the satisfaction of a groan. "As it happens, my granddaughter does have a handicap."

"So she's in a wheelchair, too?"

"I didn't say that, did I?"

I waited for more details, but Crawley gave none. So now I was moved from walking dogs to babysitting for some spoiled Veruca Salt–ish little girl.

"You will be here at ten o'clock sharp tomorrow. But first you will introduce yourself to the shower in your house, and you will dress in something presentable. You will also refrain from calling me Chuckles in front of her."

"Tomorrow's Saturday. I've got stuff to do on Saturday."

Which was actually just a whole lot of lying around, and I guess he figured that out, because he said: "Don't force me to make your life more miserable than it already is."

I finally realized who he reminded me of: the Emperor in *Star Wars*. "Fine. But right now I'm gonna walk dogs so the Schwa doesn't have to do all the work."

"You're such a Boy Scout."

"Hey!" I said. "Enough with the insults!" I hooked Gluttony to a leash, and left.

"Maybe she's like the Elephant Man."

Howie, Ira, and I hung out in my unfinished basement later that night, for the first time in a few weeks. We didn't find much to say to one another, so we resorted to our old standby, playing video games. Our current choice was "Three Fisted Fury," in which steroid-pumped opponents, having been exposed to radiation, have grown more than the usual number of arms and must battle for ultimate dominance of the world. You know—just like the movie.

It was Howie who suggested the Elephant Man theory. We had all been trying to figure out what condition Crawley's granddaughter suffered from that was bad enough for him to pay me to spend time with her.

"I mean, she's got to be ugly in some basic, unnatural way to make it worth money," says Howie.

"Maybe not," said Ira. "Maybe it's Tourette's syndrome."

"What's that?" I asked.

"It's where you have these little seizures and can't stop cursing people out."

"Sounds like most people I know." I swung at his character on the screen with my left and right arms, then caught him off guard with an uppercut from my third arm. He lost ten points of life.

"Hey," says Ira, "what if she's the surviving half of Siamese twins connected at the head, but separated at birth. Only one of them could survive, because there was only one brain between them."

"It sounds logical," says Howie. At this point his screen character sneaks up from behind and nails me with a dropkick from a leg I didn't even know he had.

"Hey, no fair—you took an extra dose of radiation, didn't you?"

I turned from Ira's bruiser, who was still dazed, and began a few roundhouse kicks on Howie's guy. "Maybe it's just something simple," I suggested, "like she's got a peg leg or something."

"Maybe two peg legs," says Howie.

"Or a peg head," says Ira. "I'd pay to see that."

"You're not the one paying—Crawley is." I spun on Ira, gave his character a double-death blow, and he was finished. Ira dropped his controller in frustration. Now it was just Howie and me. I tore into him brutally. It wasn't because I cared about beating him; I just wanted it done. Kind of like the way you finish that last piece of pizza, just because it's there.

It only took a minute for the game to be over, and my character was raising all three of his arms in triumph to the sound of canned cheers. I sighed and put down my controller. "Hey, is it just me, or is this game less fun than it used to be?"

Ira and Howie don't have an opinion. Somehow I didn't expect them to. "The new version comes out in a month. It'll be tons better," says Howie.

I nodded in agreement because I didn't want to talk about what was really going through my mind. I was thinking about bamboo. Last year, my science teacher said that when a bamboo plant is established enough, you can actually watch it growing before your eyes. I wondered if it was sometimes the same with humans—because I was feeling this weird vertigo, like I had suddenly sprouted far beyond Howie and Ira. I knew it just like I knew that no future version of "Three Fisted Fury" was going to interest me like it did a year ago.

I heard footsteps coming down the stairs, but at first glance I didn't see anybody there.

"Hey, Schwa," I said.

The moment Howie and Ira realized who it was, they picked up their game controllers and quickly started a new game, ignoring him. It made me mad, but I didn't say anything. For Howie and Ira, it was okay when the Schwa was just a plaything—just some weird object that had strayed into their airspace like a UFO—but once they lost interest in him, he was no longer welcome on their radar screen.

"I've solved at least part of the mystery," the Schwa said, ignoring Ira and Howie just as well as they ignored him.

"Which mystery?"

"Crawley's granddaughter."

At this, Ira and Howie couldn't help but show a little bit of interest.

"What did you find out?" I asked.

"Take a look for yourself."

He hands me this printout of a page he must have gotten from some old Internet newpaper archive. An old society page from the *Daily News*. It shows a picture of a baby with the caption: *Mr. and Mrs. Charles Crawley III announce the birth of a daughter, Lexis Lynn Crawley.*

As Ira and Howie huddled around me to look at the picture, Schwa got shouldered out of the way.

"Lexis?" said Ira. "She's named after a car?"

"Spelled differently," I pointed out.

"Well," says Howie, "it looks like she didn't have a peg head at birth."

In fact, it didn't look like there was anything wrong with baby Lexis at all. "Hey, wait a second," I said. "Look at the date on that article—she's not a little kid at all. She's our age."

"Hmm," said Ira. "Whatever's wrong with her, maybe she wasn't born with it."

"Maybe she developed leprosy at puberty," says Howie. "I hear that happens."

"Yeah, maybe in Calcutta or something, but not in Brooklyn."

"Maybe she traveled," says Howie, "and brought it back with her, like the flu or mad cow."

"Well," says Ira, "whatever's up with her, you'll find out soon enough." He and Howie returned to their spot on the floor and picked up their game controllers.

"C'mon, Antsy, you playing or what?"

The Schwa may have been used to being treated like he wasn't there, but it didn't mean he had to like it. I could see an anger beginning to rise in him, simmering like beef stew in my mother's Crock-Pot, which meant indigestion and heartburn were only moments away.

"Hey!" he shouted to Howie and Ira. "The ice cream man's giving out free Popsicles," he said. If they heard him, they ignored him. He got louder. "Did you hear Martians invaded Long Island?" No response. His Crock-Pot began to boil. "Tidal wave's headed for Brooklyn," the Schwa shouted at them. "We have five minutes to live."

Howie and Ira just kept on playing.

I could see what was about to happen here. It was what you call "en passant." It's a move in chess. One pawn gives an enemy pawn the cold shoulder as it moves two squares ahead. So the ignored pawn has the right to kick the rude pawn's sorry butt off the board, just because it wants to. It's the only move I know where you get busted just for ignoring the enemy.

So here I am standing in my own basement, watching Howie and Ira walking straight into an en passant. It was their way of putting our friendship to the test. *We've had enough of the Schwa,* is what they were silently saying. *Are you our friend, or are you his?*

I should have done what I always do when I'm losing a chess match: accidentally knock over the board. But the Schwa made his move before I could do a thing, cutting in front of me and advancing on Howie and Ira. I stood back and let him do it. It was his right, and I wasn't going to rob him of it. He got in front of them, blocking their view of their video game. "Hey, in case you haven't noticed, I'm here."

Ira paused the game to keep his character from getting mauled by Howie's mutant. "We know you're here," Ira says. "Now do us all a favor and stop being here."

Then the Schwa reached over and ejected the game from the system. The screen went black.

"Let's see if you notice me now!" And he cracked the game disc in half.

This was the unthinkable. All three of us stared at the Schwa in shock. The Schwa dropped the broken disc and stormed up-stairs. Howie and Ira looked at me, still in denial that the game had indeed been destroyed.

"You gonna let him get away with that?" Ira asked.

"Shut up! Just shut up, okay?" I ran upstairs after the Schwa, taking three steps at a time, not even sure what I was gonna do when I caught him. He broke my game, so a pounding was in order, right? But I didn't feel like pounding him. I felt more like pounding Ira and Howie. By the time I got upstairs, the Schwa was already out the front door. I didn't catch up with him until he was halfway to the corner, and I practically had to wrestle him until he stopped.

"What, are you totally psycho?" I shouted.

"Maybe I am!" he screamed back at me. "Maybe that's just

what I am. Maybe I'm that quiet guy who suddenly goes nuts and then you find half the neighborhood in his freezer."

I gotta admit, that one stumped me for a second—but only for a second. "Which half?" I asked.

"Huh?"

"Which half of the neighborhood? Could you make it the people on the other side of Avenue T, because I never really liked them anyway."

I could see him trying to force down a grin. "You're not funny."

"So you gonna tell me why you trashed my game?"

"You said I'd be a legend."

"What?"

"Going into Old Man Crawley's—surviving to talk about it. 'You'll be a legend,' you said. But I'm not. Not even Tiggor and the Tiggorhoids care. They've already forgotten I exist."

"Why do you even care about those boneheads?"

"It's not just them," he says. "It's everyone. I'm sick of being looked over. Shut out. And now even Crawley's forgetting about me, and picking *you* for granddaughter duty."

"So what? It doesn't look like it's gonna be much fun."

He took a deep breath. "Sometimes . . . sometimes I'm just afraid I'll end up like . . . "

But he refused to finish the thought. He left and I didn't follow him, because I knew he didn't want me to. Instead I just went back home. Dump the board. End the game. Nobody loses.

When I got back home, Howie and Ira were playing another video game.

"That guy's one egg short of a full deck," Howie says.

"You should sue," says Ira.

I tried to say something, but words failed me. I understood why the Schwa did what he did. He had stood in front of them, and still he wasn't visible. He broke the game, and even then it didn't change anything. By tomorrow Howie and Ira will have forgotten about it.

Sometimes I'm afraid I'll end up just like . . .

Just like who? And suddenly I could hear the Schwa's voice in my head. *Just like my mother.* That's what he was going to say!

"Are you gonna play, Antsy, or just stand there?"

I wanted to talk to them about what the Schwa had said, but I knew it was pointless. It was like Howie and Ira were now on the other side of thick soundproof glass.

"I'm not feeling too good," I told them. "Maybe you guys should go."

"What's wrong?"

"I don't know. Maybe I feel a case of leprosy coming on."

They stood and said their good-byes. It took a bit longer and was a bit more awkward than the usual "see ya." Maybe because somewhere deep down we all knew that this wasn't "see ya." This was more like "so long."

Are Those Your Fingers in My Mouth, or Are You Just Happy to Not See Me?

8 I put the Schwa out of my mind, which is not hard to do, as you already know. Even with his meltdown, even with the broken game disc, I woke up in the morning without him crossing my mind once. My thoughts were occupied with the mystery of Lexie Crawley. She was fourteen, not four. I wish Crawley would have told me that up front. It put a whole new spin on the situation.

"What are you all dressed up for?" my mother asked as she peered into my bedroom that morning.

"Funeral," I told her.

She studied me, trying to decide if I was telling the truth or just being my normal nuisance. "Who died?" she asked.

"Your sense of humor," I told her.

She frowned at me, and made like she was going to match wisecracks, but instead she just came into my room and straightened the knot on my tie. "You got someone to impress at nine in the morning?" she asked.

"Ten," I told her. I lifted my neck so she could get the tie just right.

"Is she pretty?"

I just hope she's human, I wanted to say, but instead I just shrugged.

Mom stepped back to admire me. "You look handsome," she said. "Just don't make an idiot of yourself."

Unless I wanted to climb on the roof again, the only way into Crawley's apartment was through the restaurant, which was closed this time of the morning. After knocking a few times on the front entrance, I went around back, where a custodian let me in. The restaurant was creepy in the off-hours. Chairs were stacked on top of tables, the floor was still wet from the custodian's mop.

I climbed the stairs to the old, unused part of the restaurant and the big wooden door of the apartment toward the back. Even before I got to the door, the dogs began to bark.

"Get out of the way, you mutts," I could hear Crawley gripe on the other side of the door. "Get back, or I swear I'll put you in the gumbo!" Then I heard all the dead bolts snap open and he pulled the door just wide enough for me to squeeze in without letting the dogs out. I was attacked by fourteen tongues before Crawley grabbed a handful of treats from his vest pocket and hurled them back toward the living room. The dogs, who knew the drill well, took off.

"Who's there, Grandpa?" I heard a girl's voice call from deeper in the apartment.

"Just the dog walker," Crawley said.

"Dog walker?" I said. "But I thought—" Crawley rapped me hard in the arm to shut me up. "Ow!"

"It's the dog walker," Crawley said again. "He's here to walk the dogs." Then he turned to me. "Where's your friend?"

Usually I was pretty quick to catch on to things, but today I was a bit behind the curve. I wasn't sure what I was supposed to say. "Uh . . . he had to go to a funeral."

"Oh, that's so sad," I heard Lexie say. At least her voice sounded nice. I could see her stepping out of the kitchen now, but Crawley kept the place so dark I couldn't see her face.

Crawley looked at me. "I guess you'll have to walk the dogs all by yourself, then," he said. And repeated, "All by yourself."

"Uh . . . sure, I guess," I said.

And then Lexie said, "I could help."

Finally I figured out what was going on here, and I felt like a moron for not catching on sooner. As soon as Lexie offered to help, Crawley smiled and gave me a thumbs-up. This was a setup. "I don't know, Lexie . . . these dogs might be too strong for you."

"Don't be ridiculous—they're no stronger than Moxie, and if I go with your dog walker, I won't even have to take Moxie along."

Lexie finally stepped out of the shadows. I didn't see anything wrong with her at all. *Tourette's syndrome,* I thought. *Any second she's gonna start cursing me out.*

Actually, she was kind of pretty. Not perfect, of course, but then I wasn't one to judge. There was something strange about her eyes. They were half closed, like she just spent an hour in Mr. Gandler's social studies class, which, by the way, is a torture I wouldn't even wish on my worst enemy.

Lexie stuck out her hand for me to shake. I had to move a few steps forward to grab her hand, and the moment I did, I figured the whole thing out.

"You're blind!" I hadn't meant to blurt it out like that, but well, there it was.

Crawley gave me a look of disgust that could spoil milk. "How very observant of you."

"Sorry," I said to Lexie, "but your grandfather had me thinking you were a mutant or something."

"Grandpa thinks everyone's a mutant." She kissed him on top of the head.

"Everyone *is*," he grumbled.

A golden retriever much calmer than the other dogs paced out from the kitchen, wearing a harness and a rigid halter. A Seeing Eye dog. "This is Moxie," she said, and I knelt down to pet him as he came to me. "He'll be jealous when we walk the other dogs," Lexie said, "but he'll get over it."

We put two dogs on leashes. Moxie whined a bit, as Lexie predicted, and I led her out.

"Shouldn't I help you down the stairs or something?" I asked.

"Why?" she answered. "Five paces, turn right, twelve paces, turn left, twenty-two steps down, then nine paces to the door."

She navigated the stairs with confidence.

We crossed the street and walked the sidewalk that lined the bay so we wouldn't have to cross any more streets. Lexie held my arm as we walked a slow measured pace, with Prudence and Envy tugging on their leashes, and I silently wished I had lifted weights more, because she was holding on to my nearly nonexistent left bicep. I kept waiting for her to make a crack about it.

"So, how much is my grandfather paying you to entertain me?" she asked.

"Paying me? Why would he be paying me? I'm the dog walker. I walk the dogs."

"Nice try, but I know my grandfather. How much is he paying you to spend time with me?"

I was going to continue denying it, but I figured this blind girl could see through anything.

"Enough," I said.

"Whatever it is, he's ripping you off," she said. "Ask for more."

"I can't do that!"

"Why not? Your time is worth at least minimum wage, isn't it? And what about an expense account? Make sure he pays when you take me out to lunch, and when you take me dancing."

"Dancing? I'm taking you dancing?"

Lexie laughed. "Well, not if you don't want to. The boy last year couldn't dance at all."

So now I was really beginning to stutter and sputter and make all those stupid noises a guy makes when his brain slips out of gear. "He's done this before?"

"I spent the summer with Grandpa. He figures if he owns all my dates, he can keep me safe from the big bad world."

It was news to me that Crawley considered me safe. In fact, it annoyed me. What had I gotten myself into here? I had never spent quality time with a blind girl before. I had never spent quality time with *any* girl. My experiences had been mostly Kmart quality, if you know what I mean. Parties were usually just Ira, Howie, and me standing on the sidelines, drinking punch and cracking jokes about the guys who actually had dates. As for the girls I had gone out with, well, it usually felt more like the hot seat on a game show. One bad answer sends you out on your butt, and the whole world's laughing at you by eight o'clock, seven o'clock Central Time.

Lexie turned toward the bay the way most people would when they wanted to take in the view, but she was taking in the salty breeze against her face. Then she said something freaky.

"Can I see what you look like?"

I wasn't sure if she was kidding or not. "How would you do that?"

"Like this." She handed me Prudence's leash, then reached up suddenly and pressed her hand to my face. I pulled back just as suddenly. Girls generally didn't touch my face, unless slapping counts.

"Sorry," she said. "If you don't want me to . . ."

"No, it's okay. I just wasn't expecting it. Go ahead. Try again." She brought her right hand to my face again—this time more slowly. Then her left hand came up. She began rubbing both of my cheeks in little circles.

"Are my zits giving you messages in Braille?"

She giggled at that, and I prayed to God that the whitehead I'd been nursing with Clearasil didn't decide it was time to blow.

Now she moved her fingers up to my eye sockets, brushing both of my brows with her thumb before checking out the bridge of my nose. "You have good bone structure," she said, which is fine for dinosaurs in the Museum of Natural History, but not exactly the compliment you want to hear.

"That's the best you can say, huh?"

"Good bone structure is important," she said. "No matter how handsome or pretty you think you are, without bone structure to back it up, it doesn't mean a thing."

I let her continue, closing my eyes as she gently pressed her thumbs against my sockets, perhaps testing to see whether or not there was a brain behind my eyeballs.

"You have very nice eyes," she said.

Her fingers slipped down the side of my nose and began to travel the rim of my nostrils, which, I have to tell you, felt just a little too familiar. Then, before I could say anything about it, her fingers were brushing gently across my lips. It tickled. I was glad she couldn't see how much I was blushing, but I wondered if she could feel the heat rising to my face.

"Seen enough?"

"Almost." And then—God's honest truth—she pushed her fingers just the slightest bit between my lips, and started to move them back and forth across my teeth.

"I fink oo sood shtop now," I said.

"Hmm," she said, ignoring me. "You've got braces."

This was not going well. I wanted to be anywhere but there at that moment. Then she said, "I like braces. It gives a person *texture*."

Having a girl's fingers explore the texture of my dental work was uncharted territory for me. What did this mean? Did it mean we were going out? Was this like the blind version of "first base"? Or was this some other sport altogether—a sport I didn't know how to play? What if this was like cricket, which I watched once and it made no sense to me. So here's this girl with her fingertips on my teeth, which I guess is first base in a cricket match, and I'm wondering what happens if she wants to find other textures in there.

Then she took her hands away. I took a deep breath of relief. "So," I said, "do you like what you see?"

She smiled. "Yeah. Yeah, I do."

I wondered if I would get a turn now, but I was afraid to ask.

"Hi, Antsy!"

The Schwa caught me totally by surprise and I jumped. I had no idea how long he had been standing there watching. "Jeez—do you have to do that?"

"I was wondering when you'd say something," Lexie said.

I turned to Lexie. "You knew he was there?"

"Of course. I could hear him breathing. What did he call you?"

"Nothing," I said. "Just a nickname."

"She saw me!" said the Schwa. "She actually saw me!"

"She didn't see you, she's blind."

"But she knew I was here!" The Schwa was getting all excited now. "Hey, Antsy, maybe we can do another set of experiments with Lexis. See if she's immune to the Schwa Effect. Maybe it's genetic—her grandfather usually notices me, too."

Lexie smiled. "*Antsy?* He called you *Antsy?*"

I threw up my hands. This was the classic three's-a-crowd scenario, and right now three felt more like Times Square on New Year's Eve. "Schwa, could you just go and walk some dogs?"

"I got all day."

"Aren't you going to introduce us?" asked Lexie.

I sighed. "Lexie, meet the Schwa. Schwa, meet Lexie."

"Calvin," he said. "Pleased to meet you."

By now Prudence and Envy were both getting restless. We walked them back home, and I took them upstairs alone. When I came back outside, Lexie was touching the Schwa's face.

"Hey!" I shouted, running back to them.

"I wanted Lexie to see me," the Schwa said, "like she saw you."

"What if she doesn't want to see you?"

Lexie's eyebrows furrowed as she keyboarded across the Schwa's face. "Hmm . . . that's interesting."

"What?" the Schwa asked. "What is it?"

"I don't know. It's like . . . It's like I can't get a clear impression. Your face feels . . ."

"Invisible," I suggested.

"No," said Lexie, searching for the right word. Now she moved her fingers across his face more intently than she had searched mine. And although she touched his lips, she didn't check out his teeth. If she did, I would have thrown a hemorrhage, although I can't really say why.

"His face is . . . pure," she said. "Flavorless—like sweet-cream ice cream."

The Schwa smiled. "Yeah? My face is like ice cream?"

"Sweet cream," I reminded him. "It has no taste."

"Yes, it does," said Lexie. "It's just very subtle."

"Nobody likes it," I said.

"It's my favorite," Lexie answered.

The Schwa only grinned, and threw a disgustingly happy glance in my direction.

Now let's be clear on something here. I had only just met Lexie, and she wasn't really my type. I mean, I'm Italian, she's blind. It was a mixed relationship. But seeing her fingers on Schwa's face . . . I don't know, it did something to me.

The two of us had lunch down in Crawley's restaurant. Lobster on the house. Schwa, in his slippery way, appeared at the table and tried to squeeze in, but I was ready for him. I quickly brought down two dogs for him to walk, and no sooner had I put the leashes in his hands than the maître d' threw a conniption fit about health codes, and quickly shooed Schwa and the dogs out the back way.

"You're friend's funny," Lexie said after he was gone.

"Yeah," I said, "funny in the head." Right away I felt this unpleasant stab of guilt for turning on the Schwa like that.

Lexie smirked, and for a moment I forgot she was blind, because I knew she was seeing everything.

Maybe They Had It Right in France Because Getting My Head Lopped Off by a Guillotine Would Have Been Easier

9 Life went from being a bad haircut to being an algebra exam. In algebra, things only make sense once you're done, there are no shortcuts, and you always have to show your work. The problem becomes more complicated the second you add a new variable. I mean, solving for x was hard enough, but with me, Lexie, and the Schwa, too, I had to solve for $x, y,$ and z. When things get that complicated, you might as well just put down your pencil and admit defeat.

The thing is, the Schwa was not just your typical variable—he was like i, the imaginary number. The square root of negative one, which doesn't exist, yet does in its own weird way. The Schwa was on the cusp of being there and not being there, which I guess is why he clung so tightly to Lexie and me.

The Schwa called me the next morning to invite me over for lunch. I was busy working on my social studies report, the history of capital punishment—which wasn't a bad topic, since it involved beheadings and electrocutions—but it was Sunday.

Sunday and homework go together like oil and water, which, by the way, is what they boiled criminals in during the early Middle Ages. Oil, not water, although I didn't realize the hot water I would find myself in by accepting the Schwa's lunch invitation.

Mr. Schwa wasn't wearing his painter's clothes when he answered the door, but the jeans and shirt he wore did have little paint splotches all over them. He also held a butcher knife.

"Can I help you?"

If those paint splatters on his clothes had been red, I probably would have run off screaming.

"I'm Calvin's friend, Antsy."

"Of course you are. I think Calvin's at school. . . but then, if he were at school you'd be at school, too, so maybe he's not."

"It's Sunday."

"Of course it is! Come on in."

I took another look at the knife, and went in against my better judgment.

The Schwa was in the kitchen, rearranging the Post-it notes on the fridge. "Hi, Antsy," he said in such good spirits I wondered if he had won the Lottery or something.

"Have a Coke," he said, shoving the can into my hand. "My dad's making franks and beans for lunch."

Now that he had been reminded of what he had been doing, Mr. Schwa returned to the kitchen.

"C'mon," said the Schwa, "there's something I want to show you." The Schwa dragged me to his room, where his box of zip-locked paper clips sat on his bed.

He reached in and gingerly pulled out a little bag. "I'll bet you've never seen anything like this before!" The thing inside did not look like a paper clip. It might have once been a brass brad or something, but now it was broken, and all crusty black. The Schwa held the bag like the little thing inside would turn to dust in seconds.

"It looks like a bird turd."

"It's an old-fashioned paper fastener." He smiled so wide, it was like his head was on hinges, like one of those ceramic cookie-jar heads. "It's from the *Titanic*."

I looked at him, sure he was about to burst out laughing, but he was serious.

"Where do you find a paper clip from the *Titanic*?"

"I wrote to the Nova Scotia Maritime Museum six times," he said, "because I knew they had a ton of *Titanic* junk stored away—mounds of stuff that wasn't interesting enough to put on display. Finally I faked a letter from my doctor, telling them I had a rare brain disorder—"

"—and your last brain-fried wish was for a paper clip from the *Titanic*?"

The Schwa nodded. "I can't believe they bought it."

"I don't think they did. I think they sent it just to get rid of you."

The smile kind of shrunk from his face, and he looked down. "So, do you want it?"

"Me? After all you went through to get it, why would you give it to me?"

"Well, if you don't want this one, you can have another one." He dug into his box and came up with one little bag after another. "How about this one from Michael Jordan's first basketball contract—or this one? It's rumored to have been clipped to the results of an alien autopsy. I got it on eBay."

"Whoa, slow down." I grabbed one of his hands, and the box

flipped off his bed, dumping little packets all over the floor.

"Sorry, Schwa."

"No problem."

If there's one thing I've learned, it's that there's no free lunch—and no free paper clips either. We stood there looking at each other. "So what is it you want?" I asked him.

He sighed one of those breathy sighs like a convict does moments before his execution—not that I've ever seen that.

"You gotta let me have her, Antsy."

"Her? Her who?"

"Lexie! Who else? Please, you gotta let me!"

He grabbed me, pleading. I shook him off. "She's a person, she's not a thing. I can't 'let you have her.'"

"You know what I mean." He got up and started pacing in short U-turns, like a condemned man waiting for a pardon from a governor who was probably out playing golf. "We were made for each other! Don't you see? Invisible guy/blind girl—it's perfect. I even read it in a book once."

"You read too many books. Go see some movies. In the movies invisible guys never get the girl. Instead they usually turn evil and die horrible, painful deaths."

"Not always," he said.

"Always. And besides, you're only half invisible, so, I dunno, maybe you should look for a girl who's blind in one eye."

He punched me hard in the arm, and I punched him back, matching his force. We both refused to rub our aching arms, even though they hurt. For a second I wondered whether this would swell into a full-on fight.

"Hey," I said, "Lexie does what she wants—and besides, I was the one Crawley hired to hang with her, not you."

"But, but . . ." The Schwa's mouth was opening and closing like a goldfish. "But she said I'm sweet-cream . . ."

"Big deal. I'm Italian gelato, and there's only room for one scoop on the cone." Which technically isn't true, but he got the point.

Then the Schwa invokes the friendship clause.

"Antsy, you're my best friend," he says. "I'm asking you as a friend. Please . . ."

Like I said, I was in hot water, because whether I like it or not, I got a conscience. But I also got a selfish streak, and once in a while it kicks in before the water starts to boil.

"Forget it," I told him.

Then Mr. Schwa burst happily into the room. "Okay, boys, lunch is ready. It's franks and beans!"

He left, never noticing our argument, or the paper clips on the floor. I knelt down to pick up the bags of clips. "Do these go in any order?"

"Put them in any way you want." He left for the kitchen, letting me pick up all the clips.

We didn't talk much over lunch, and said nothing about Lexie. The Schwa cleaned his plate, but if you ask me, he looked like a man eating his last meal.

The Schwa was not giving up. For a guy famous for not being noticed, he was suddenly everywhere. Somehow he managed to walk Crawley's dogs three at a time without being dragged down the street like a human dogsled. That meant he was done with the job quick enough to barge in on anything Lexie and I were doing.

I was coming up with all this clever stuff to do with her—it amazed me how clever I could be when a girl was involved. It actually gave me hope that maybe I had latent superintelligence that was activated by girls, like the way the Incredible Hulk was activated by anger.

One afternoon, I had this bright idea of playing "Name That Texture," which consisted of us challenging each other to identify unusual objects just by feeling them.

"In school we do a lot of tactile learning," she warned me. "I know the whole world by touch."

Because she had an advantage, I chose really weird things for her, like a geode, and a Pisher Plastic replacement kneecap. She chose normal household things for me, because the only thing I knew by touch was my bathroom light switch in the middle of the night. And even then I turned on the fan half the time by mistake.

As soon as the Schwa showed up to walk the dogs, Lexie invited him to play, too. I didn't move to give him a place to sit, but he made room anyway, so I glared at him.

"Why the dirty look, Antsy?"

He knew why. He had only said it to inform Lexie I was mad-dogging him.

"Come on," said Lexie, "we're all friends."

I put my blindfold on, and the game quickly became an exercise in embarrassment. I had just mistaken a corkscrew for a Swiss Army knife when I heard Crawley roll by. I peeked out from under my blindfold to catch him sizing me up in his own disapproving way. "The boy cannot correctly identify a corkscrew," he said. "Don't let this moron dull your intelligence, Lexis."

I grinned at him and said, "Send in the clowns!"

Old Chuckles was not amused.

After Crawley rolled away and I had handed Lexie her next mystery object, she whispered so her eagle-eared grandfather couldn't hear. "Sometimes I think my grandfather died long before I was born."

"Huh?" I said. It was such a weird thing to say.

"You want me to think this is a quarter," Lexie said of the object in her hand, "but it's a Sacagawea dollar." She was, of course, right.

Once we heard the door to the old man's bedroom close, Lexie said, "The way he lives in this stuffy cave. It's not really living, is it? That's why I come to stay with him. My parents would much rather I stay somewhere else when they go out of the country, but I want to come here. I'm still working on changing him."

While the Schwa pondered his object, I pondered what she had said. I didn't think Crawley could be changed. My dad once told me that people don't change when they get older, they just get *more so*. I imagine that when Crawley was younger, he was the kind of kid who always saw the glass half empty instead of half full, and had a better relationship with his dog than with the neighborhood kids. In seventy-five years of living, half empty became bone-dry, solitary became isolated, and one dog became fourteen.

"Saltshaker!" said the Schwa.

"Wrong. It's the queen from a chessboard," said Lexie.

"Your grandfather is who he is," I told her. "You should just live your own life, and let him live his. Or *not* live his, I guess."

"I disagree," said the Schwa. "I think people can be changed— but usually it takes a traumatic experience."

"You mean like brain damage?" I asked, then immediately thought about the Schwa's father and was sorry I said it.

"Trauma comes in many forms," Lexie said. "It changes you, but it doesn't always change you for the better." She handed me my next object; something like a pen.

"Well, if it's directed trauma," said the Schwa, "maybe it could change you for the better."

"Like radiation," I said. They both waited for me to explain myself. This was easier said than done, on accounta the intuitive part of my brain was three steps ahead of the thinking part. It was like lightning before thunder. But sometimes you see lightning and the thunder never comes. Just like the way I'll sometimes blurt out something that sounds smart, but if you ask me to explain it, the universe could end before you get an answer.

"We're listening," Lexie said.

I fiddled with my object, stalling for time. "You know, radiation . . ." And for once it all came to me—what I meant, and what I was holding. "Just like this . . . laser pointer!" I must have known in some subconscious way all along.

"I get it," said the Schwa. "Radiation can be like a nuclear missile, or it can be directed, like a medical treatment that saves your life."

"Yeah," I said. "When my uncle got cancer, they used radiation therapy on him."

"And he lived?" asked Lexie.

"Well, no—but that's just because he got hit by a garbage truck."

"So," said Lexie, "what my grandfather needs is *trauma therapy*. Something as dangerous as radiation, but focused, and in the proper dose."

"You'll figure it out," I told her.

"Yes," she said, "I will."

I gave her the plastic kneecap, but I could tell her mind was no longer on the game. She was already thinking of a way to traumatize her grandfather.

"Maybe if we put our heads together," the Schwa said, "we'll come up with something quicker."

I squirmed. "Three heads are a crowd," I said. But whatever Lexie's opinion was, she kept it quiet.

That Friday night I had Lexie all to myself, since the Schwa's aunt came over every Friday night. I took her to a concert in the park at an outdoor amphitheater.

The music was salsa—not my favorite, but that was okay. Concerts have a way of making music you don't regularly like, likable. I guess it's because when the people around you really like it, some of that soaks into you. It's called osmosis, something I learned about in science—probably by osmosis, since it isn't like I was listening. I was listening to the music, though, and so was Lexie. I watched the way she moved to it, and I didn't even feel self-conscious watching her because she couldn't see me doing it.

We had great seats—right smack in the middle. The handicapped section. I have to admit I felt guilty—not only because I wasn't handicapped, but because Lexie was the most unhandicapped handicapped person I'd ever laid eyes on.

"Are you having fun?" she asked when the band took a break.

I shrugged. "Yeah, sure," I said, trying not to sound like I was having as much fun as I really was, because what if she took my real enthusiasm for fake enthusiasm?

"I like this band," Lexie said. "Their sound's not all muddy. I can hear all seven musicians."

I thought about that. I had been watching them for more than half an hour, and now that they were off the stage, I couldn't tell you how many musicians there had been.

"Amazing," I said. "You're like one of those mentalists. You can see things with your mind."

She reached over to pet Moxie, who sat next to her in the aisle, content as long as he was petted every few minutes. "Some people are good at being blind, others aren't," and then she smiled. "I'm very good."

"Great. We'll call you the Amazing Lexis."

"I like that."

"And now," I announced, "the Amazing Lexis, through her supersonic skills of perceptive-ability"—she giggled—"will tell me how many fingers I am holding up." I held up three fingers.

"Um . . . two!"

"Wow!" I said. "You're right! That's amazing!"

"You're lying."

"How do you know?"

"There's only a one-in-four chance that I'd get it right—one-in-five if you counted your thumb as a finger—so the odds were against it. And besides, 'lie' was written all over your voice."

I laughed, truly impressed. "The Amazing Lexis strikes again."

Lexie grinned for a moment, and I noticed how her smile fit with her half-closed eyes. It was like the face you make when you're tasting something unbelievable, like my dad's eggplant Parmesan, which is poison in anyone else's hands.

Lexie reached over to pet Moxie again. "Too bad Calvin couldn't come with us."

"Oh," I said. "Yeah, right." I probably would have gone the whole night without thinking about him once, and now I felt a little guilty about that—and annoyed that I felt guilty—and irritated that I was annoyed. "Why would you want the Schwa on a date with us, anyway?"

"This *isn't* a date," Lexie said. "People don't get paid to go on a date."

She thought she had me there. "Well, you're not supposed to know I'm getting paid—and since you know and are still letting me take you out, it *is* a date."

She didn't say anything to that. Maybe she just couldn't argue with my logic.

"There's something . . . unusual about Calvin," she said.

"He's visibly impaired," I told her. "Observationally challenged."

"He thinks he's invisible?"

"He *is* invisible . . . kind of."

Lexie screwed up her lips so they looked kind of like the red scrunchy she wore in her hair, then said, "No, it's more than that. There's something else about him that either you don't know or you're just not telling me."

"Well, his mother either disappeared in Waldbaum's supermarket or got chopped up by his father, who sent pieces to all fifty states. No one's really sure which it is."

"Hmm," Lexie said. "That's bound to have an effect on a person, either way."

"He seems okay to me."

"He's very sweet," Lexie added.

"*Ripe* is the word," I said. "He's gotta start wearing deodorant."

The lights in the amphitheater started to dim, and the crowd began cheering for the band to start.

"Maybe you should walk the dogs," Lexie said.

"Huh?"

"I said maybe you should walk the dogs, and Calvin should be my escort."

I wasn't expecting that. It hit me in a place I didn't know was there. All I could think of was one of those medical shows. They're operating on some poor slob, they accidentally nick an artery, and he starts gushing. "We got a bleeder!" the surgeon yells, and everybody comes rushing to the operating table. Nobody was rushing to me, though.

"Sure," I said. "If that's what you want."

The band began to play, and I quickly wiped away the tears I was bleeding, even though I knew she couldn't see them.

Lexie confronted her grandfather the next morning, telling him she knew that he paid boys to hang around with her. I showed up at Crawley's that afternoon, determined to quit before I got fired, but Crawley didn't give me the satisfaction.

"You are a miserable failure," the old man told me. "You couldn't even keep our financial arrangement a secret."

"She already knew," I told him.

"How could she already know? What do you take me for, an idiot?"

"Sometimes, yeah."

He grunted, then threw a chew toy at Fortitude, who was

gnawing on his shoe. The toy bounced off the dog's nose, and she went for it, trotting off happily with the toy in her jaws.

"Apparently, whatever you did, it disgusted my granddaughter enough that she'd rather be with that Schwa kid than with you. You are hereby demoted to dog walker again."

"Who said I'm doing anything for you anymore?"

"*You* did," Crawley said calmly. "You accepted twelve weeks of community service."

"Well, now I unaccept it."

"Hmmph. Too bad," Crawley said. " I was actually beginning to think you had some personal integrity."

I grit my teeth. I don't know why it mattered what he thought of me, but it did. He was right; I was a miserable failure—even at quitting.

"Do you want me to walk the dogs now or later?"

"Walk them at your leisure," he said, and rolled off. For once he didn't gloat over his little victory.

I went to get the leashes and spent my afternoon trying to think of nothing but walking dogs.

Earthquakes, Nuclear Winter, and the End of Life as We Know It, over Linguini

10 My parents had a fight on the day I got demoted to dog walker. Maybe it was no worse than other fights they had over the years, but I noticed it a whole lot more. Maybe because seeing the Schwa's sorry home life made me more tuned in to my own.

I heard them even before I walked in the door. They were screaming at each other like the Antonoviches two doors down, who would end our dependence on foreign oil if you could harness the sheer vocal energy of their fights.

"It's the Big One," Frankie said when I came in the door. "I estimate eight-point-six on the Richter scale. Better hold on to something." He pretended to watch TV while listening to the fight.

Christina crouched by the kitchen door, sticking her nose in, and writing in her diary. "It began at five-eleven P.M.," she said. "Thirty-seven minutes straight, so far."

"Red sauce?" I heard Mom yell. "I'll give you red sauce!"

We all knew the Big One was a clear and present danger. For

years we hoped the pressure could be released through smaller tremors, and for years it had worked. I was beginning to think maybe the Big One wouldn't come at all.

"If it wasn't for me, you'd all starve!" Mom yelled.

"At least we'd be out of our misery!" Dad shouted back.

The Big One was all about food. Mom was no slouch when it came to cooking—but, like I said, Dad stood in a league by himself. No parent I know—mother or father—could whip up dishes the way my dad did, but he didn't often get the chance, because the kitchen was Mom's. Dad might have been the Vice-Vice-President of Product Development for Pisher Plastics, but Mom was the Empress of Bonano Food Productions, and I pity the fool who challenges her reign.

Dad was that fool. It was his destiny.

Well, if the Big One was tonight, they picked the wrong day to have it. I had just walked fourteen dogs, been dumped by a blind girl, been dumped *on* by her grandfather, and right now I wanted a cold soda.

"Antsy, don't go in there," Frankie warned. "We ain't got any body bags."

I figured I could slip in and out unnoticed. The Antsy Effect was nowhere near as potent as the Schwa Effect, but in my own family, it worked just as well.

I pushed my way past Christina, who was scribbling her life away in the diary, logging her impressions of the battle for future generations.

The scene was weirdly dramatic. Like something out of Shakespeare. Dad waved a spatula in the air as he spoke, making him look like a swordsman, and Mom spoke with her hands so much, it looked like karate.

"I'm tired of eating your family's lousy, tasteless recipes," Dad said.

"Tasteless recipes? My grandmother's rolling in her grave!"

"It's from indigestion."

She threw an artichoke at him, and he batted it away with the spatula.

I went to the refrigerator, took out a Coke, and then something very strange happened. I flashed to Howie and Ira playing "Three Fisted Fury," ignoring the Schwa. Anger began to boil up inside me. Yeah, I could get in and out of that kitchen unnoticed, but suddenly I didn't want to. I didn't want to ever again. I had a right to be noticed.

"Excuse me," I said, loudly. "If you two are just going to argue all night, I'll cook dinner; otherwise we'll all be rolling in our graves from parental starvation."

"Don't you open up a mout like that!" Mom said.

"Go back to the living room," Dad said. "This isn't your problem."

"Bullpucky!" I said, which isn't actually the word I used, but I'm in a much better mood now than I was then.

When she heard that, Mom drew in a breath kind of like the way the ocean sucks back before a tidal wave. "What did you say?!"

"I said it's time to eat. If you wanna fight, why don't you lose a few teeth and go on a daytime talk show?"

Mom glared at me, and crossed her arms. "Do you hear this?" she says to Dad. "Where do you learn this disrespect, huh?"

"You don't learn disrespect," I told her. "You're born with it."

"Just keep digging that hole deeper, Antsy," Dad said. So now all their anger had turned away from each other and was aimed at me. There was awesome power in being the center of fury.

"You want to earn your dinner, smart mout?" Mom says. "You tell us—who makes a better fra diavolo sauce. Me or your father?"

It was a stupid question, because who really cared, and yet I knew the answer was critical. The old Antsy would have found some way to distract them from the argument and, failing that, would have said something to keep the peace, like "Mom's is better with pasta, Dad's is better with meat" or "Dad's is spicier, but Mom's is heartier." An answer would have held everything together and would have eventually gotten things back to normal.

Then it occurred to me exactly what my place in this family was, and had always been. In spite of my wisecracking, pain-in-the-neck ways, I was the clip that held things together. Unnoticed. Taken for granted. Okay, maybe I'm giving myself too much credit here, but I'd be damned if I was gonna keep on being the family paper clip.

"You gonna answer us or not?"

"You want the truth?" I asked.

"Yes, of course."

"Okay, then. Dad makes the best fra diavolo sauce."

Stunned silence from the both of them. They hadn't wanted the truth. We all knew it. Suddenly I wasn't playing by the rules. "And come to think of it, his alfredo sauce rocks, too. What else do you want to know?"

Dad put his hand to his head like he had a headache. "That's enough, Anthony."

Mom nodded and pursed her lips into a thin red line. "Okay," she said. "Okay, that settles it, then." I didn't like the calmness of her voice. She walked over to the range, took the big pot of sauce she had made, and in one smooth motion dumped it down the drain. A cloud of steam rose and curled like a hydrogen bomb had gone off in the sink.

"You make dinner, Joe." She stormed out of the house, leaving us all in nuclear winter. Once she was gone, Frankie pulled me aside and glared at me. "You see what you did?"

Dad did cook us dinner that night. He had to go to the grocery store to get his ingredients, so dinner wasn't ready until nine. He made us veal rollatini, better than you'd get in the best Italian restaurants. We all ate and said nothing to one another. Not a thing, not even "pass the salt," because it didn't need salt. It was, at the same time, the best and the worst meal I had ever sat down to.

When it was done, we all did our own dishes and left the kitchen spotless. Dad made a plate of leftovers and put it in the fridge. I knew it was for Mom, but he wouldn't say it.

Frankie and Christina went to their rooms, but I hung around in the kitchen a bit more while Dad cleaned the pots.

The clip is gone, I thought. *The pages are flying like confetti. What a moron I am.*

"So what happens now?" I asked.

"I don't know, Antsy."

The fact that he didn't know scared me more than anything else that night. Was our family so fragile that this could tear the foundations loose?

"It seems like such a little thing," I said.

"The biggest things always seem like small things," he told me.

I stayed up as long as I could that night, waiting to hear the front door open and Mom walk in, but I fell asleep before I heard it. In the morning, I woke up feeling no better than I had the night before. Mom wasn't in the bedroom, and Dad had already left for work. I went downstairs slowly, afraid she might not be there. What would I do if she wasn't? What would that mean?

I don't know, Antsy.

Parents were supposed to know the answers, and even if they didn't, they could usually fake it really well. I wanted to hate my dad for not knowing, but I couldn't hate him. That made me want to hate him even more.

I came downstairs, and Mom was in the kitchen. I had to hold on to the wall, as if the Big One was having an aftershock. I took a deep breath and went in. She was drinking coffee by herself, like they do on those commercials for fancy flavored coffee.

"Are you having breakfast before you go to school?"

"What is there?"

"Cornflakes, Raisin Bran. There may be some Froot Loops left, if Christina didn't make a pig of herself."

Most of the time Mom would get the bowl, or the box or the milk. She would always do something to be a part of the meal. Today I did the whole thing myself. It just didn't feel right.

When I got the milk from the refrigerator, I noticed that the plate of food Dad had left was gone. The plate had been washed by hand, and now sat in the drying rack. I knew it shouldn't matter. I knew it was just a little thing—but the image of that plate on the rack stayed with me all day. Like Dad said, sometimes the little things are the biggest things of all.

And for the life of me I couldn't figure out whether Mom had eaten the food on that plate or had put it down the disposal.

I sat by myself at lunch on Monday. I hadn't been sitting with Howie and Ira for a couple of weeks now. Used to be we were inseparable, but cliques are like molecules: They bind together in Mr. Werthog's little test tube until you add something new. Then they all break up and recombine into something else. Sometimes you get these things they call "free radicals," which are atoms that aren't bound to anything else, floating free. That was me now. I didn't mind it at first, because it left open a whole lot of possibilities, but after this past weekend, radical freedom didn't feel so good.

I'm sure the Schwa was there, blending in with the Formica tables, but I wasn't about to look for him. Right now I was hating him the way you hate the other team when they shout, "Two-four-six-eight, who do we appreciate?" after humiliating you in a shutout. The Schwa found me, though. He plopped his semi-invisible self down across the table from me.

"Do you mind? I'm eating, and it's hard enough to keep this crud down without having to look at you."

"I just wanted to thank you, Antsy. That's all."

"Thank me for what?"

"Lexie told me everything. She told me what you did."

"What did I do?"

"Don't play dumb," he said. "You told her you didn't want to be her escort, and said that I'd be better at it. I can't believe you'd do that for me. No one's ever done anything like that for me."

I just sat there with gravy dripping down my chin. "She told you that?"

The Schwa grinned. "She's teaching me Braille," he said proudly. "It's really cool." He glanced at my plate, noticing I had eaten my peach cobbler first, so he scooped his onto my plate. "If you ever want *anything*, all you have to do is ask."

Pamela O'Malley passed by just then, with a few friends walking so close it was a wonder they didn't trip over one another's feet. "Hey, Antsy," she said, "how come you're eating alone?"

The Schwa gave me that "some people" look.

"Maybe I like it that way," I said. She twittered with her friends and walked off.

"It's okay," the Schwa said. "Who needs to be seen when you can be *felt?*"

The Youngest Doctor in Sheepshead Bay Gets Held Hostage When He Least Expects It

11 Being felt.

That means a lot of things, doesn't it? And I'm not talking about the dirty stuff you probably think I mean. My mind isn't in the sewer all the time, all right? I'm talking about having your presence felt. In that way, I guess I'm not all that different from the Schwa.

Now I had made my presence felt in my own family by refusing to be the peacekeeper. If that was a good thing, it sure didn't feel like it. The problem is, once you've made yourself felt, there's no going back to being unnoticed, as much as you might want to. Instead of ignoring me, Frankie was suddenly noticing every little thing I did, wondering why I did it. Christina started asking me questions about things, like I was the smarter brother. Dad was now confiding in me about things that were really none of my business, and Mom started treating me like I was actually a responsible human being. It was all very disturbing.

"There's no future in plastic," Dad said to me one day out of the blue.

"Sure there is," I told him. "People will always need a plastic something or other."

"We can only hope," he said.

"What does Mom think?"

"Mom doesn't work for Pisher."

I was fishing for news from the battlefront, but he gave me none. The battlefront had become more like a demilitarized zone. They kept this chilly emotional distance. I think I liked it better when they fought.

The thing is, Dad might have built Manny to be indestructible, but he himself was not. Neither was Mom. This was a stress test I wished would just end.

I didn't know what I'd say to Lexie. I was sure to run into her at Crawley's apartment eventually, but I hoped maybe she would just leave the room and pretend she didn't know I was there until I had leashed up the dogs and left.

I wasn't so lucky.

A week after being replaced by the Schwa as her official escort, Lexie herself came to answer the door. She pulled it open wide, letting out four dogs, three of which nuzzled me for affection, but the fourth one, Prudence—who was always a loose cannon—bolted, and headed straight down the stairs. Not the back stairs we always take to get out, the grand staircase that led right down to the middle of the restaurant, where people were eating an early dinner.

"Great," I said. "She'll probably pull a lobster right off of someone's plate."

"I need your help," Lexie said. At first I thought she meant to get the dog, but then I heard Crawley shouting and groaning from inside the apartment, over the sound of barking. Lexie's voice was all warbly, and I could tell she was panicked. "He fell in the shower," she said. "I think he might have broken his hip again."

I stepped in, closing the door behind me. Let the waiters deal with Prudence, they were probably used to it. "Did you call 911?"

"They're sending an ambulance, but he won't let me near him. He won't tell me anything. I don't know what to do."

I tried to hurry back to the master bathroom with her, but she couldn't hurry. She moved slowly, and methodically, never bumping into anything, but never quickening her pace. It was the first time I'd ever seen her handicap be a hindrance.

Crawley was sprawled on the shower floor, clutching a towel over himself.

"Get out!" he said when he saw me.

"There's an ambulance on its way," I told him.

"I don't need an ambulance. Just leave me alone."

It was terrible to see him like this. He had always been such a powerful presence, even in his wheelchair. Kind of like Roosevelt, you know? But lying there on the floor, twisted in that awkward position, he seemed frail and helpless. I reached over to help him shift into a more comfortable position, but he swatted my hand away. "Get your lousy hands away from me, you dumb guinea!"

Whoa.

He had called me lots of things, but never the *G*-word. I

didn't know what to make of it, but now wasn't a time I could really get angry. He tried to move by himself, and yowled in pain, letting loose a whole dictionary of cusswords.

Lexie, standing at the door, grimaced. "What happened? Did he fall again? Tell me, Anthony! Tell me everything that's happening."

"Nothing's happening. He tried to move, but couldn't."

"Is he bleeding?"

"No."

Then she hit her eyes with her palms and grunted. It was weird, but I knew exactly why she did it. It was frustration at her own blindness. She was smooth and confident when the world cooperated, but accidents were almost as uncooperative as her grandfather. "Isn't there something we can do?"

Yes, there was. I went over to the medicine chest and opened it to reveal a whole pharmacy of medication. I quickly scanned the labels.

"What are you doing now?" Crawley asked.

"You need something for pain, and an anti-inflamatory," I told him. I knew about that from the injuries we've had in my own family.

"So you're my doctor now?"

"Yeah, Dr. DumGuinea, and I'm sending you one helluva bill." I found what I was looking for, checked the labels for dosage and expiration date, and pulled out a pill from two different vials. Then I filled a glass with water from the sink and cautiously approached Crawley.

"What's that?"

"Lodine and Vicodin," I told him. "They prescribed these for you when you first broke your hip, right?"

"I don't need it!" He pushed the glass away, spilling half the water on my shirtsleeve.

"Fine. Suit yourself." I put the glass down on the counter with the pills, making sure he could see them. If he looked at them long enough, maybe he'd change his mind.

"They're coming!" Lexie said. She heard the sirens long before I did. The last time I heard sirens here, it was the police coming for the Schwa and me.

When Crawley heard the approaching sirens, he groaned. "I don't need this today!"

There was a knock at the door, and I hurried off to let in the paramedics. Instead, it was the Schwa, with an out-of-breath waiter holding Prudence by the collar.

"Hi, Antsy!" the Schwa said brightly, like this was the happiest place on Earth. "What's up?"

"Don't ask."

I ran back to the bathroom, where Lexie still stood by the threshold, her grandfather yelling at her every time she tried to get closer.

"Anthony! Make her get out of here!"

"Lexie, maybe you should just go sit down—at least until he calms down."

Exasperated, Lexie left for the living room.

"He's lying on the floor," the Schwa said, like I didn't know.

"I'll have those pills now," Crawley said.

I handed him the pills and glass. "Careful, that Vicodin can be habit-forming."

He gave me a nasty glare and took them.

The Schwa was trying to get up to speed, but not quite making it. "Uh—shouldn't someone help him up?"

As if things weren't crazy enough, when Lexie let the para-medics in, Prudence bolted again, followed by at least three other dogs.

The paramedics freaked and put their hands in the air, which is the worst thing to do around an excited dog, because it thinks, in its pint-size dog brain, that you have a treat in your hand, and so up the dog goes, planting its paws on your chest. Now imagine that multiplied by ten.

"He's this way—in the bathroom," I told them, but they were cornered by the sins and virtues and weren't going anywhere. "C'mon, haven't you ever seen Afghans before?" I had to use the old man's trick of throwing a handful of treats clear across the room to free the paramedics.

When medical professionals took over the situation, I thought I could be out of this little drama. I figured Crawley would go off, complaining all the way, with Lexie in tow, and Schwa and I would be left to walk the dogs. Crawley, however, threw a curveball.

The paramedics got him up onto the gurney, and as they were wheeling him out, he grabbed my arm. "Anthony, you come with me."

"What, me?"

"Is there another Anthony here?"

"I'll come, Grandpa," said Lexie, already getting Moxie ready for the journey.

"No. You will stay here with Calvin and walk the dogs."

"I want to come with you!"

The paramedics rammed right into the Schwa, knocking him flat on his butt. The dogs, who had been calming down, began barking again.

"Sorry, kid, we didn't see you."

"Anthony—come!" said Crawley.

I turned to the Schwa and Lexie, holding back the dogs as they wheeled Crawley out. "I think my job description just changed again."

They let me ride in the back of the ambulance with him as they ran red lights and took the wrong side of the road halfway to Coney Island Hospital.

"Why did you want me to come?" I asked Crawley. "Why not Lexie?"

"I don't want her to see me like this."

"She can't."

"Don't be a smart-ass, you know what I mean." He shifted positions and grimaced. "Tell them you're my grandson at the hospital, and weasel your way into the ICU. You're good at weaseling."

"Thanks, I think."

The paramedic checking Crawley's blood pressure threw me a quick glance, but didn't say anything. I guess whatever went on at the hospital wasn't his business.

Then, when the ambulance pulled to a stop at the emergency room, Crawley grabbed my arm again. His nails dug into my forearm, although I don't think he did it to hurt me, and he said: "Don't let them leave me alone."

I sat beside him in a little curtained emergency-room cubicle, listening to him complain about everything from the antiseptic smell to the flickering fluorescent lights that "could send some-one into a seizure." Everything in the hospital was a lawsuit waiting to happen, and he was prepared to bring in his lawyers at any moment.

I called my parents to tell them where I was. Never open up a conversation with your mother with the words, "I'm at the hospital."

"Oh, my God! Did you get hit by a car? Oh, my God! Is anything broken? Oh, my God, Antsy, oh, my God!"

She was so loud, I had to pull the phone away from my ear, and Crawley could hear every word. It was actually a comfort to hear my mother showing concern, so I let it go on for a moment before I stopped her and told why I was at the hospital.

"Mr. Crawley's really shaken up. I guess I'll be here for a while."

"Is he okay?" Mom asked. "Is he gonna live?"

"Not if I can help it."

Crawley let out a single loud guffaw at that. It was the first time I had ever made him laugh.

"Call when you need a ride home," she said.

"Don't worry, I'll get a cab."

At the mention of that, Crawley's eyes got a little wider, and his lips pursed a little tighter. After I hung up he said, "You leave when I tell you to leave. I'll pay you time-and-a-half for overtime."

"Not everyone in the world does things for money, okay?"

"You do."

"Well, not all the time."

"Good. Then I won't pay you."

"Okay, I'm leaving."

"Aha!" he said, pointing his finger at me.

Now it was my turn to laugh.

Crawley glanced out the little opening in the curtain. Doctors and nurses whooshed past every minute or so, but never whooshed in. "Hospitals are the greatest failure of civilization," Crawley proclaimed.

"You're not the only patient. They'll get to you eventually."

"So will the coroner."

I looked at him for a moment, remembering what he had been like when they wheeled him in. As soon as they had opened the door to the ambulance, he had covered his face with both hands, like a vampire afraid of the light of day, all the while calling to me in a panic.

"Why are you so scared to be alone?" I asked him.

Crawley ignored the question so I tried another.

"Why am I here instead of Lexie?"

Crawley took a long moment to weigh his answer, then sighed. This was a good thing, because when people sigh, it usually means they're about to tell the truth. A sigh means it's not worth the energy to lie.

"The more Lexie knows, the more she'll tell her father— my sson," Crawley said. (He spat it out, like it was a four-letter word instead of three.) "I don't want my sson to know anything. He's already convinced that I need to be in an 'assisted-living facility.' An old folks' home."

"Well, you're an old folk."

"I'm venerable, not elderly." And at my puzzled expression he said, "Look it up."

"I don't need to. I'm sure it's just a word that's supposed to make 'old' sound good, like they say 'restroom' when they really mean 'bathroom,' and they say 'bathroom' when they really mean 'toilet.'" Then I added, "It's called a euphemism. Look it up."

He waved his hand at me. "I don't know why I waste my breath. You couldn't possibly understand what I mean."

"I think I do."

I thought he'd just wave his hand at me again, but to my surprise he was actually listening—which meant I had to find a way to put into words what I was thinking. I began slow, just in case I flew into some speed bumps that sunk my train of thought.

"Right now everybody knows you as kooky Old Man Crawley, with fourteen dogs in his window and enough power to shut down the egg supply to half of Brooklyn."

He grinned. "They still remember the eggs, do they?"

"Who could forget? But once you get put in a rest home, you'll just be some old fart playing checkers and waiting for the aquacize instructor. You won't be a mysterious force to be reckoned with anymore. And that's scary."

He looked at me for a long time. I figured he was generating a really good insult, but instead he said, "You're slightly brighter than I gave you credit for."

"You know, your son will find out about this. Lexie will tell him—she probably already has."

"Just as long as I'm out of here and back in my apartment when I face him." Then he added, "I just hope Lexie's all right with that lackluster friend of yours."

"I'm sure your granddaughter and the Schwa are having a great time. They probably got their hands all over each other's faces or something." The image of that was just too disturbing. I had to stand up and pace in the little space, peering out of the curtains to see if the doctor was coming. The greatest failure of civilization. Maybe Crawley was right.

"My granddaughter is very upset with you."

This was news to me. "What does she have to be upset about? She was the one who dumped me for the Schwa."

Crawley looked at me square in the eye. "You're a moron."

"I thought you just said I was brighter than you gave me credit for."

"I stand corrected."

As it turns out, Crawley had fractured his hip again. It wasn't bad, but a fracture is a fracture. He couldn't keep the news from his "sson," but as Lexie's parents were still in Europe, their war was limited to transatlantic phone calls. They insisted he spend time in a nursing home, and he told them what they could do with their nursing home. In the end, Crawley agreed to hire a full-time nurse, but in the meantime was happy to torment the nurses at the hospital.

From his hospital room, Crawley commanded Lexie to go to school the next day rather than visit him, and he raised such a stink she did as she was told. My parents, on the other hand, let me take off school that day, since I had been up all night with Crawley, and that gave me time to take the subway down to the Academy of the Blind before school let out.

At the end of their school day, the students left with precision and care, unlike the mob scene at most other schools. Many students were escorted by Seeing Eye dogs, parents, or nannies. A few older ones went out alone with white canes tapping the pavement in front of them. Some of Lexie's schoolmates seemed well accustomed to their state; for others, it was a serious hardship. I never imagined there was such a range in how people handled being blind.

The strangest thing of all was the way drivers used noisemakers to guide their student to the car. Some clicked, some whirred, some whistled—and no two were the same. It was amazing, because every kid found their way to the right car with just a couple of toots or clicks.

Moxie spotted me before I spotted Lexie, and he brought her to me.

"Moxie? What's wrong, boy?"

"Hi, Lexie."

It only took an instant for her to recognize my voice. "Anthony, what are you doing here? Is my grandfather all right?"

"Yeah, yeah, he's fine. I'm here because I needed to talk to you."

"So you came all the way here? Couldn't you wait till I got home?"

"Yeah, I guess, but I didn't want to."

Someone pulled up to the curb, rolled down the window, and blew a slide whistle.

"Do they do that at all blind schools?" I asked Lexie.

"I don't think so," she said. "This one is just weird." She turned her head slightly to the side. "I hear my driver further up the street. C'mon, you can ride home with me."

She led me to a black Lincoln—a car service that the Crawleys had hired to take Lexie to and from school. The driver had a Pakistani look about him, and rather than using a plain old noisemaker, he was playing the harmonica. Badly.

"My father started him off with a kazoo. I gave him the harmonica because it's so much more dignified. I figure he might actually be able to play by the end of the school year."

We got in the car and sped off, with Moxie lying across our feet.

"Your grandfather says you're angry at me."

"He told you that?"

"Yeah, and I think I've got a right to know why. I mean, you dumped me in the middle of a concert, and now you're the one who's angry at me?"

Moxie sensed a little anger on my part, and he barked. It was the first time I had ever heard him bark.

"Dumped you? Is that what you think?"

"No, I guess not. I guess you just fired me. That's just as bad. So now I want to know why you're the one who's angry. If anyone should be mad, it's me."

"I'm not angry. I'm just . . . disappointed."

"Why?"

"Because *you* dumped *me*."

"Now you're just playing games with me."

"No, I'm not," she said. "As long as you were being paid, we couldn't really be dating, could we? I even said that at the concert, didn't I?"

"Yes, but—"

"So if Calvin is my paid escort, my grandfather gets what he wants, and then you could ask me out for a *real* date." And then she added, "But you didn't."

My jaw swung open like Wendell Tiggor in math. Words failed me.

"I swear," said Lexie, "you sighted people don't see anything unless it's staring you in the face." And then she leaned forward and planted a kiss square on my mouth. It was a perfect hit, like she had a radar lock on my lips. Then she said, "Is there anything unclear about that, or do you need a Hallmark card?"

I looked around, self-conscious as anything, but there was no one to see us but Moxie and the Pakistani driver, who kept his eyes on the road like it was the hardest level of a video game.

"I guess I get the picture now," was all I could say. Then a nasty little thought surfaced to ruin the moment.

"What about the Schwa?"

"Calvin's my friend," Lexie said. "He'll understand."

"I don't think so. *He* thinks you're going out."

"Don't be silly. No, he doesn't."

"Hey—you don't know him like I do."

"He's my escort. We have fun together. He knows there's nothing more to it than that."

"You don't get it, do you? If we start going out, it will crush him. He's one of us handicapped sighted people who believes what he sees."

Lexie pulled her shoulders back, getting all offended. "I think I'm a much better judge of character than you think I am."

"All I'm saying is that we can't do this to him."

"So you don't want to go out with me?"

I sighed. "I didn't say that either."

A Horror Movie Blow-by-Blow, with the Undisputed Queen of the 3-B Club

12 Unlike my parents, I don't know much about cooking. According to them, the only recipe I know is a recipe for disaster. I actually have a few of them. Here's the latest: Take one blind girl who's not nearly as insightful as she thinks she is, add one Italian ham, sprinkle generously with Schwa, then put in a pot and turn up the heat.

I asked Lexie out to dinner, and she suggested we go to a movie first. It didn't occur to me that the movies with her would be an altogether different experience. Since I was no longer her paid escort, I had to shell out the money for it myself. I didn't mind. It felt like an accomplishment.

I knew the Schwa would have a cow if he knew about the date—more than a cow, he'd have a whole herd—but I put him out of my mind, for once allowing the Schwa Effect to work in my favor. I forgot him and let myself have a good time with Lexie.

Usually you took a girl to the movies so you wouldn't have to talk, and so you'd be in a position to put your arm around her shoulder and, God willing, make out. But going to the movies with Lexie was like taking an Honors English class.

"Okay . . . now she's walking toward the air lock," I announced. We were about ten minutes into the movie and I hadn't stopped talking yet.

"How is she walking?"

"I don't know—like a person walks."

"Is she strolling, meandering, stalking?"

"Storming," I said. "She's *storming* down the hallway toward the air lock."

The music flared, the air lock hissed open, and the audience screamed.

"Is that the monster?" Lexie asked.

"Yeah."

"Describe it."

"It's big, and bluish green."

"Don't use colors."

"Uh . . . okay. It's crusty like a lobster, and spiny like a porcupine. You know what that is?"

"I'm blind, not stupid."

"Right." I had forgotten about "tactile learning."

"What's happening now?"

"She tries to run , but the air lock closes. The monster backs her against the door. Its claws move forward. She opens her mouth to scream, but she can't because she knows screaming won't make a difference."

"Shh!" said someone in front of us.

"She's blind—you got a problem with that?"

The monster did its thing, and the audience shrieked, their voices blending into the squishing, crunching sound effects.

"What did the monster do?" Lexie asked.

"You don't want to know."

"Yes, I do!" She licked her lips. "Every little detail!"

By the time the movie was over, I felt like I was stumbling out of a day of state testing.

"Don't worry," Lexie said as we left arm in arm, "I won't ask you to describe the food on my plate."

At dinner, however, she asked the waitress for a Braille menu.

"Are you kidding?" I told her. "This is just a burger place; they don't have Braille menus."

"He's right," said the waitress.

"Then I'd like the manager to come out and read me the menu," she said.

"I can read it," I told her.

"No, I want the manager."

The waitress snapped her order booklet closed. "Sure, hon," and she went off to find the manager.

"You like giving people a hard time, don't you?"

Lexie grinned. "Only when they're blind to the blind."

In a few moments the manager walked out. No—*strided* out. This was one of those places famous for, like, fourteen thousand different burgers on the menu, and Lexie charmingly insisted that the manager read every single one of them, like it was his catechism. When he was done, she gave him the phone number of a place where he could order Braille menus.

That's when I think I fell in love.

"What if he'd refused to read you the menu?" I asked after the manager was gone.

"Then I'd sic the Four-S club on him."

"Don't you mean Four-H?"

"No, Four-S. It stands for the four senses other than sight. It's a club at my school. We have contacts with the mayor's office and the *New York Times,* and we organize pickets in front of antiblind establishments."

"You should call yourself the Three-B club," I told her. "Blind Ball Busters."

She laughed.

"I'll bet you're the leader."

She didn't deny it. "I'm a force to be reckoned with."

"Just like your grandfather."

When it came to body language, I wasn't exactly bilingual, but still I could tell by the way she shifted that she wasn't too pleased by the comparison. "I meant that in a good way," I told her. "I mean, it's like we all get our raw materials from our families—but it's up to us whether we build bridges or bombs."

"What are you building?" she asked.

"I don't know. A fast car, maybe."

"To go where?"

She stumped me for a second, until I sidestepped the question with this: "It's the road that matters, not the destination."

I gotta admit, I impressed myself with how well I could pretend to be clever, until she said, "You're so full of crap!"

I laughed so hard practically my whole Coke sprayed out of my nose.

"Tell me something about you that I don't know," she asked.

"Okay, let's see . . ." I scanned through all the things she didn't know about me, which was about everything.

"I got two webbed toes on each foot."

"Ooh! A mutant!"

"Yeah, and if you ask to feel them, I'm out of here."

"Well, maybe when we go swimming someday."

"Okay, your turn."

"I'll tell you about Moxie," she said. "Most people think it's for 'moxie,' the word that means 'gutsy,' but it's not. You see, when I was little and I got sick, that's what I used to say to my parents—'Moxie! Moxie!' Because they always gave me amoxicillin, and I knew it was supposed to make me feel better. So when they brought me a Seeing Eye dog, I called him Moxie, because from the moment I had him, I felt better about being blind."

"That's nice," I said, avoiding the more common "that's cool," because her story deserved more respect than that.

"You know, I wasn't born blind," she said. "I fell out of my stroller when I was a year old, and hit the back of my head on the curb."

Just imagining it made me grimace. "The *back* of your head?"

"That's where the visual cortex is. It's kind of like a movie screen at the back of your brain. Without it your eyes can work just fine, but there's no place to show the movie."

"Wow," I said, wishing I knew a more respectful word for *wow*.

"I'm lucky. It happened early enough that I was able to compensate and adjust. It's harder the older you are."

"Do you remember seeing at all?"

It took a while for her to answer that one. "I remember . . . remembering. But that's as close as I can get."

"Do you miss it?"

She shrugged. "How can you miss what you don't remember?"

Whether she liked it or not, Lexie had a bit of her grandfather in her when it came to bending the world to suit her. She could wrap the world around her finger like a yo-yo string and play with it to her heart's content. She definitely toyed with me on a regular basis, but that was only because she knew I liked being her yo-yo.

She also knew all the right strings to pull once she finally settled on how to give her grandfather "trauma therapy."

"It took lots of money," she told me, "and lots of favors, but it will be worth it because it's exactly what my grandfather needs to break him out of his shell." Then she said, "Of course I can't tell you what I'm planning, but I promise when it happens, you'll be in on it."

This was one of those times I didn't like being toyed with. I kept no secrets from her, except of course for the secrets I kept from everybody, so why couldn't she tell me what she was planning?

"Aw, please?" I begged, feeling stupid, but heck, if she could give Moxie a treat when he begged, maybe her compassion extended to two-legged creatures. No such luck.

"It's no use," she said, putting her palm against my lips to shut me up. "You'll find out when you find out." Then she added, "And don't ask Calvin, because he won't tell you either."

I moved her hand off my face so I could gape in deeply offended disbelief, and it really annoyed me that she was blind, because my deeply offended gape fell on deaf ears.

"You told the Schwa, but you won't tell me?"

"Calvin can keep a secret."

"So can I!"

She laughed. "You? You're like Radio Antsy—all news, all

the time. If I told you, even the dogs would be barking it by morning."

"Very funny."

So the Schwa and Lexie were sharing things that Lexie wouldn't share with me. So what. I put my arm around her in a way that only a boyfriend can. That was something she and the Schwa didn't share. I hoped.

Okay, I admit feeling pretty jea-lousy about it (that's feeling jealous and lousy all at once). For a few seconds . . . well, maybe more than just a few seconds, I wished the Schwa would really disappear.

Later I'd feel real guilty about that.

A Russian Train, a Pulsing Vein, and My Mother's Bag of Snails

13 Mrs. Greenblatt, who lived two doors down from us, was not blind, but she was extremely nearsighted. I figured she never had laser surgery on her eyes because it would have been physically impossible to implant the Hubble Telescope in her cornea, which is what she needed. Her nearsightedness wasn't really a problem, except for the fact that she often mistook me for my brother, and lately even my father. However, things came to a head one day. Literally. I wasn't home when it happened, but I heard the story from so many different people it was like watching on one of those multi-angle DVDs. About three in the afternoon, while Mrs. Greenblatt was trimming her hedges, she came across a human head wedged in the bushes. She died of a heart attack about three times, then ran inside to call the police. I'd love to hear *that* 911 tape.

By the time the police arrived, half the neighborhood had heard the screaming and came over to investigate. The police went into her yard and came out with a head, just like Mrs. Greenblatt said. She claimed to be having several more heart attacks, until she found out the head wasn't human. It was the head of Manny Bullpucky—slightly dented and singed from our attempt to blow him up, but otherwise completely intact.

My brother Frankie got it back for us, and that evening I snapped it onto Manny's body, then called Ira and Howie to let them know. We began to plan his death one more time.

"Can I come to one of your demolition sessions?" Lexie asked when I told her about it. "It sounds like fun."

"Sure," I told her, although I was doubtful about how much she would get out of merely hearing Manny's destruction. I figured it would be good to have her there, because things were strained between Howie, Ira, and me. Killing Manny was the only thing we had in common anymore.

We met at about four o'clock on Saturday. Our crime scene was the elevated subway station in Brighton Beach, which was pretty deserted on weekends this time of year.

"I don't like this place," Howie says as we climbed the steps. "I mean, is it *elevated?* Or is it a *subway?* It can't be both. It gives me the creeps."

We figured we could get away with making Manny a subway victim here, because Brighton Beach is mostly Russian these days, therefore normal laws, rules, and space-time physics don't always apply. Besides, the police are more worried about the Russian Mafia than about a bunch of kids. You don't want to mess with the Russian Mafia. They make Mob guys like John Gotti look like Mr. Rogers. In Brighton Beach it's always a beautiful day in the neighborhood, and if you don't agree, you may end up sleeping with the beluga.

So anyways, Ira's got his camera filming Manny, who's slouching on a bench, looking like a postapocalyptic crash-test dummy. "With what this guy's been through, he could be a superhero."

"We shoulda done this on a weekday, during rush hour," Howie says. "The more people on the train, the higher gross tonnage. Maximum breakage potential."

"Yeah, but we could derail it," I said, for like the fourteen thousandth time. "Better an empty train than a crowded one."

That's when Lexie comes up the stairs with Moxie, and someone else. It takes me a moment to realize it's the Schwa.

I hadn't invited him. Not intentionally, of course—he just slipped my mind like always. It hadn't even occurred to me that he would come with Lexie. That's how far out of my mind he had slipped. It spooked me out, the way it spooks you out when you can't remember something simple, like your phone number, or how to spell your middle name. I heard someone say that when that happens, it means the brain cells that held the information just died, and your brain's gotta find the information in some backup file. This was not a good thing, because if the Schwa Effect was actually killing all the brain cells that remembered him, I could end up as brain-dead as a Tiggorhoid.

"Hi, Antsy," said the Schwa.

"Hi, Anthony," said Lexie.

The Schwa introduced Lexie, and everyone was polite enough, although Ira and Howie made secret cracks about how they look together—then snickered like a couple of fifth graders. I couldn't get past how awkward this all felt. But the Schwa didn't seem to feel awkward at all. He stood there grinning like an idiot, and clutching Lexie's arm like he was escorting her to the Academy Awards.

"Who's gonna do the honors?" Ira asked.

Usually Howie volunteered to throw Manny to his death, but right now he was too busy staring at Lexie, waving his hand in front of her face. "So you don't see anything at all?" he says. "Not even shadows?"

"Nope."

"When you're blind, you're blind," I said.

"Not always," Howie says. "There are blind people who can read large-print books."

"That's 'legally blind,'" Lexie explained. "I'm not legally blind."

"Yeah," I said, "she's illegally blind. Now can we get on with this?"

"Lexie," said the Schwa, still holding her by the elbow, "would you like me to guide you to a bench?"

"That's all right, Calvin, I'd rather stand."

Ira and Howie shared a look that could have meant any one of a dozen nasty things, then Howie turned to the Schwa. "So, Schwa, done any good vanishing tricks lately?"

While Howie taunted the Schwa, Lexie whispered my name to Moxie, and he led her over to me. "It doesn't sound like you're having fun," she said.

"How do you know? I've barely said a thing."

"That's what I mean."

"Well, I've got a lot on my mind."

A train crashed past on the far track, and Lexie reached up to touch my face.

"Don't," I told her. "Not in front of the Schwa." But she couldn't hear me over the roar of the train. As soon as the train had passed, she leaned in close and whispered, "I really had fun the other night. Let's go to the movies again." Then she kissed me.

When I looked up, the Schwa was standing right behind her.

I had no idea how long he had been there, or what he had seen. All I know is that the sky up above was a clear ice blue, and so were his eyes. Piercing ice blue.

Usually Lexie knows exactly where everyone's standing, but not all the time. I could tell she had no idea that the Schwa was right there. "Moxie, bench." Moxie led her over to a bench, and she sat down.

The Schwa waited until she was gone, just staring at me with those icy eyes. He seemed calm, but there was this vein pulsing in the translucent skin of his forehead. "Why did she kiss you?"

I shrugged. "Don't read too much into it. That's just the way she is."

"No," he said. "She doesn't kiss me like that. I mean, sometimes she kisses me on the forehead like . . ."

He looked over to see Lexie stroking Moxie. He licked her face, and she gave him a kiss. On the head.

"Like that . . ." the Schwa said. Until that moment I suppose he had been legally blind to the situation, but now it was spread out for him in large print. I knew it would have to happen eventually, but I was hoping I'd get lucky, and the world would get struck by a comet or something first.

"I'm sorry, Schwa, okay? I'm really sorry."

He responded with icy eyes, and a pulsing vein.

Far off a horn blew, and I could see the headlights of a train coming around the bend.

"It's an express!" yells Howie, all excited. "It's not gonna stop here—it won't even slow down! Maximum breakage potential!"

I didn't need a second invitation. Anything to look away from the Schwa's eyes. I grabbed Manny by the scruff of his neck, dragged him to the caution line, and hurled him into the path of the approaching train. I caught a quick glimpse of the conductor's surprised face before Manny disappeared beneath the wheels. Car after car raced past, and in a few moments the train was gone.

"Did it work?" Lexie asked. "What happened?"

Long story short, Manny Bullpucky was not stronger than a locomotive. Manny didn't just break, he shattered. He was hit so hard, pieces of him flew out of the station, to the street below. There were body parts around Brighton Beach for weeks, which was nothing new, only these parts were plastic. The Q express train had sent Manny to the great recycling bin in the sky.

"I'm gonna miss him," Ira said as he packed up his camera and turned to go.

When I looked for the Schwa, I didn't see him anywhere, and for the life of me I didn't know whether he had left or just blended into the station. It wasn't until Lexie asked me to escort her home that I really knew he was gone.

"I don't understand," she said. "That's not like him to leave without saying good-bye."

"You don't get it, do you?" I said. "How could you be so . . . so . . ."

"So what?"

"Never mind. Forget I said anything." I reached over and took Moxie's harness, putting it gently into her hand. "Better hold on to Amoxicillin," I told her. "I have a feeling you're gonna need him to make you feel better."

"How could you have done that to him?" I asked Lexie after I had gotten her home.

She glared at me. Not with her eyes, but with her whole face, which was worse. "In case you've forgotten, you did it, too."

I knew she was right, and it just made me angrier. We sat in the living room of her grandfather's apartment, listening to the sudden November downpour. Crawley's nurse, who had already made it clear that she was a cat person, had walked the dogs in the rain because I hadn't shown up on time to do it. Now the whole apartment was toxic with wet dog, and the nurse gave me dirty looks every time she passed by.

"I thought he understood that we were friends," Lexie said.

"I don't believe you. Just because you couldn't see the dopey love-look on his face doesn't mean you couldn't hear it in his voice."

Lexie was getting teary-eyed, but I wasn't feeling too sympathetic.

"Maybe I just didn't want to hear it, okay? Maybe I wanted a little bit of both of you. Is that so terrible?"

Then something occurred to me. "You've never really gone out with boys before, have you?"

"What does that have to do with anything?"

By her tone of voice, I knew it was true. "A lot more than you think," I told her. See, I know girls and guys who have become masters of manipulation when it came to dating. Instinctively I knew Lexie wasn't one of those slippery types. Yes, she had manipulated us, but there was an innocence about it. Like she got tossed too many boys to juggle, and so she was doing it not because she enjoyed it, but because she didn't know what else to do.

She didn't speak for a long time. She just wiped her eyes with the back of her hand, then reached down to pet Moxie. Moxie was pushed away by the sins and virtues, who wanted attention as well, and that just frustrated her even more.

"I tend to intimidate the boys at my school," she finally said. "I'm very outgoing, and most of them aren't. You see, it's a very exclusive school, and a lot of the kids have been much more sheltered than me. I guess they just don't know what to make of me."

"What about your other escorts? The ones before me and the Schwa?"

"They were always older," she said, "and to them it was just a job. Besides, they were always church boys—you know, boys who are so weirdly polite, you always feel like you're in church when you're with them. My escorts were always boys who were safe. . . which is why I was so surprised that my grandfather chose you."

"He must be going senile."

"I heard that!" Crawley shouted from his bedroom. A few of the dogs perked up at the sound of his voice and ran off to torment him. Served him right for eavesdropping.

"So I guess we were like training wheels," I said to her.

"What?"

"You know, like on a bicycle. One on either side. Me and Schwa. Dating wheels."

"I can't ride a bicycle. I don't know what you're talking about."

But I think she did.

"Calvin must hate me," she said, nervously picking at her fingernails.

"He doesn't hate you. He just feels a little worked over, is all."

"How about you?"

"No, of course I don't hate you."

She reached out and touched my cheek. I thought about how that felt. I'll bet no one had ever touched the Schwa's face until Lexie had. Touch is a freaky thing when you're not used to it. It makes you feel all kinds of things.

I guess I didn't respond the way she wanted, because she took her hand away. "What happens now?"

I had to think about my answer because my own feelings hadn't settled yet. Were we going to keep seeing each other? I wanted to. Being with her made me feel like Anthony instead of Antsy. But my selfish streak had run its course, and my conscience kicked in with a vengeance. It would never be right if I did this at the Schwa's expense.

"I think you're going to have to ride without training wheels for a while," I told her.

"So then . . . what are we? Are we friends?"

I took real care in my answer. "I'm your grandfather's dog walker," I told her. "Let's start from there."

Remember the Schwa.
Go to his house.
Go talk to him.
Remember the Schwa.

After I left Lexie, I kept repeating things about the Schwa over and over in my mind. I didn't care how many brain cells it killed trying to think of him, I knew I had to go see him, or call him, or something. I couldn't let him sneak out of my mind like he always did. Right then I knew how bad he must have been feeling.

Remember the Schwa.

Go talk to him.

But when I got home, Dad called a family meeting. Everyone was there but Mom. He had us sit at the dining-room table, where we never sat. The dining-room table was for holidays and taxes, that was it. As I sat down, I suddenly realized I didn't want to hear this.

"We all need to have a talk," he said. "Because things will be changing around here."

I swallowed hard. "Changing how?"

Dad sighed. It was the truth sigh. I hated the truth sigh more than anything in the world right then. "Well, for one, I'm going to be cooking a lot more."

"And?" said Frankie.

"And?" said Christina.

"And your mom . . ."

"What about Mom?"

Dad sighed again. "Your mom is taking a cooking class three nights a week."

Us kids looked at one another, waiting for more, but that's all Dad offered.

"That's it?" I said. "She's taking a cooking class?"

"And she's looking for a job. Probably part-time at first."

Nothing from any of us for a few moments.

"It's a French cooking class," Dad continued. "Now I want you to listen to me, and listen to me closely." He looked us all in the eye to make sure he had our attention. "When she cooks something, you have to tell her EXACTLY what you think of it. *Capische?* Don't pull any punches. If it's the foulest thing you've ever tasted, tell her the truth. You've got to be honest about it. Just like Antsy was the other day."

"That ain't right," says Frankie.

"I'm scared," says Christina.

"I know it's going to be difficult for a while," Dad said, "but we'll get used to it."

And suddenly, out of nowhere, I found myself bursting into tears. Don't ask me to explain it, because I can't. I didn't even try to stop it, because it was like one of those floods that washes cars away. I guess my brother and sister were freaked out by it, because they took off, leaving me alone with Dad.

"It's okay, Anthony," he said, putting his hand on my shoulder. "It's okay." He called me Anthony instead of Antsy, and for some reason that just made me cry even more.

Finally my eyes cleared, and I was looking down at the little drops of tears on the polished wood table.

"I should have used a coaster," I said. We both laughed a tiny bit.

"Wanna tell me what that was about?"

I sighed the truth sigh. "I thought you were gonna tell us that you guys were splitting up. You know? Getting divorced." It hurt to say the word aloud. Almost got me crying again.

Dad raised his eyebrows then folded his arms and looked at

his reflection in the shiny wooden table. "Not today, Antsy."

"So what about tomorrow?"

He offered me the slimmest of grins. "Tomorrow we eat French."

The next morning I woke up with the nagging feeling that there was something I was supposed to remember, but I had no idea what it was. It was like Lexie's sight—a memory of a memory.

It was Sunday. Had Lexie and I made plans to do something before yesterday's disaster? Was that what I was supposed to remember?

Mom was out early that morning and came back from the supermarket with a strange collection of groceries that included a bag of snails.

"Those French!" she said. "They can figure out ways of making anything edible."

The sight of the snails absolutely terrified Christina. I helped Mom unpack, just so that I might have some early warning as to what else was in store for us come dinnertime.

I moved a bunch of recipe cards she had clipped together so I could unpack the last bag, and the clip fell off. The clip bounced on the linoleum floor with a tiny little clatter that I could barely hear over the refrigerator hum.

A paper clip.

I stood there with the recipes in one hand and half a pound of pig brains in the other, staring down at the clip like an idiot. I suppose only something that small, that unnoticeable, could remind me of the Schwa.

"Antsy, what's wrong?"

I handed her the pig brains. "Gotta go!"

I hurried to the door, but before I left I grabbed a pen and wrote on my palm in big blue letters: SCHWA'S HOUSE, just in case the Schwa Effect kicked in and I forgot where I was going.

More Than I Ever Wanted to Know
About the Schwa's Childhood

14 I rode my bike at top speed and got to the Schwa's house in just a few minutes. As I ran up to the door, I could hear Mr. Schwa playing guitar inside. I rang the bell three or four times until he finally came, answering the door with a friendly grin.

"Hi, is Calvin home? I have to talk to him."

He looked at me strangely, and for a single, terrifying moment, I thought he'd say, *Calvin who?*

But instead he said, "Sure, he's in the bedroom."

I went in to find he wasn't in his bedroom at all.

"Hmm," said his father brightly. "Maybe he's not home after all."

"Don't you even know when your own son is home?!"

"Yes," he said, not so brightly this time. "Mostly."

I looked in every room, trying to figure out where he might have gone. Then the guitar started up again, and that was the last straw. I went to the living room, to see Mr. Schwa playing and humming to himself like he didn't have a care in the world. Well, he needed to have some cares.

"Do you even know if Calvin came home last night?"

He looked at me confused. "Calvin always comes home. Why wouldn't he come home?"

"For all you know, he could be floating facedown in Sheepshead Bay!"

He stopped playing, but didn't look at me.

"Or maybe he's with his mother," I said. "What do you think? You think maybe that's where he is?"

"That's enough, Antsy," said the Schwa. "Leave him alone."

He stood in front of the brick fireplace, wearing a dark red sweater. Blending in. Always blending in.

"*There's* Calvin," said Mr. Schwa. "He's standing over there. No worries."

"Where've you been?" I asked.

"Here and there," he said. "Mostly here."

His father returned to playing guitar.

"Dad," said the Schwa, "Marco and Sam will be here at noon to pick you up. You have a painting job in Mill Basin."

"Okay," he said.

I went with the Schwa into his room, and he closed the door. The curtains were drawn, and the only light was what little spilled over the edges of the closed blinds.

"It looks like you're turning into Old Man Crawley."

"I quit yesterday," the Schwa said. "Crawley made a big stink, threatened to get my dad fired and all, but I didn't care. My dad's friends would never fire him anyway."

"I thought you might quit," I said.

"I'm quitting you, too, Antsy."

"What's that supposed to mean?"

"It means you can stop pretending to be my friend now. You don't have to feel sorry for me."

"I don't! Well . . . actually I do, but only *because* I'm your friend. I'm not pretending about that."

"It doesn't matter."

"I'm sorry about what happened with Lexie. I thought you should know I'm not going out with her anymore."

"That doesn't matter either. You can go now. Really."

He sat there, waiting for me to leave, but I didn't. I didn't say anything else back to him either. They say action speaks louder than words, but so does inaction. Sitting there like a rock was the strongest statement I could make about our friendship.

The Schwa watched how I didn't move. I think it made him uncomfortable because he looked away. "You shouldn't feel sorry for me," he said. "You know, Buddhists believe the state of nonbeing is the perfect place to be."

"You're not a Buddhist."

He looked at me, thinking for a moment. "I'll tell you something, Antsy. I'll tell you something you've always wanted to know—but if I tell you, you have to promise to believe it."

"If that's what you want, Schwa, sure. I promise."

"Okay, then I'll tell you a story . . ."

. . . And there, in that darkened room, where I couldn't see the color of the sky or anything else in his eyes, the Schwa told me his deepest, darkest memory.

"I learned about the Schwa Effect when I was five," he said, "although I didn't have a name for it then. I didn't have a name for it until you gave it one, Antsy. But I was five when I first re-alized that something was wrong.

"I can't remember what my mother looked like, but I do re-member the last time I saw her. We had gone to Kings Plaza, and she bought me clothes. I was about to start kindergarten, and she wanted me to be the best-dressed kid in school. She wanted me noticed.

"I remember she was sad. She had been sad for a long time, so I didn't think it was anything unusual. On the way home we stopped at the supermarket to pick up something for dinner. I sat in the little kiddie seat of the shopping cart, and we went down all the aisles. It was this game we played—even when she just had to pick up a few things, she would take me down all the aisles, and I would try to name all the food. Ketchup. Pick-les. Spaghetti.

"We got to the frozen-food aisle. Outside it was a summer day, but in there it felt like winter. I can still feel that chill. Then she took her hands off of the cart. 'I'll be right back,' she said. 'I forgot the beef.' She left, and I waited. Peas, corn, broccoli. I started naming all the frozen vegetables. String beans, spinach, carrots—and for a moment—just the tiniest moment, I forgot why I was there. I forgot who I was waiting for. I forgot *her*. Just for a moment—that's all. And by the time I remembered, it was too late.

"But I didn't know that yet. So I sat there in the little kiddie seat, strapped in, freezing, and kept waiting. Lima beans, cauliflower, asparagus. She wasn't back yet. Not in five minutes, not in ten. There were no more vegetables left to name.

"That's when I started crying. Just whimpering at first, then getting louder. Crying out for anyone to help me. Someone, please find my mommy. She's just in the next aisle. I cried and cried, and you know what? You know what? *No one noticed.*

"There I was, crying my eyes out, alone in a shopping cart, and people just walked on past like I wasn't there. Not the other mothers, not the·stock clerks, not the manager. They didn't see me, they didn't hear me. People just grabbed their food and went. And that's when I knew it would be like that always. Someday there'd come a time for me, too, when no one remembered me—not a soul. And on that day I'd disappear forever, gone without a trace. Just like her."

I listened to his story with my heart halfway up my throat. I couldn't imagine what it would be like to sit in a shopping cart, alone in a crowd of people, waiting for a mother that never came back.

"Schwa," I said, slowly, "people don't disappear just because no one remembers them."

"If you can't remember them, how would you know? Think of the tree, Antsy. The tree falling in the forest. If nothing and no one is there to hear it, then it doesn't really make a sound, and if nothing and no one remembers you, then you were never really there."

I couldn't say anything. In the dim shadows of the room, and with what I already knew about the Schwa, it almost seemed possible.

"But . . . you *were* there, Schwa—someone *did* notice you in that shopping cart, otherwise you'd still be sitting there today, blocking people from getting their lima beans."

"I don't remember that—all the rest of that day is a blur. The next thing I remember for sure, though, was being in the police station with my father, answering questions and watching him fill out papers. I kept quiet mostly. I got the feeling that the cop didn't even know I was there, and it made me mad. So I took something. Something he wouldn't notice, but something that would prove I was there. When he picked up the missing persons report, all the pages slipped out and flew all over the ground, and I laughed. The cop didn't know why the pages had fallen, but I did."

"The paper clip!" I said. "You took the paper clip!"

"When we got home, Dad acted like everything was normal. It was before his accident, but he acted like he couldn't remember her. From that moment on, he never talked about her. Her pictures disappeared from the walls, and soon everything that reminded me of her was gone. Everything but this."

Then he reached beneath his mattress, fished around a bit, and pulled out a little plastic bag. "I don't keep this one with the others," he said. He handed me the bag and I held it like it was a diamond. As far as I'm concerned, that paper clip was the most valuable thing I'd ever held in my life.

"I don't care what you say, Schwa—you're not going to disappear."

"That's right, Antsy, I won't. I'm gonna make sure of it. I'm gonna do something that will make me so visible, no one'll ever forget."

"What are you going to do?"

I couldn't see if the Schwa was smiling, but somehow, I don't think he was.

"You'll see."

Vortex in Aisle Three—
Can Someone Please Clean Up
the Ectoplasmic Slime?

15 I had no idea what the Schwa had in mind, but I didn't like his eerily calm tone of voice. It haunted me all the way home. It was what you might call a "blaze of glory" calm. I started to think of that old cartoon where Daffy Duck gets no respect,. so, to prove he's a better act than Bugs Bunny, he swallows a few sticks of dynamite, guzzles a can of gasoline, and then swallows a lighted match.

"Yeah," he says as he floats up toward the pearly gates, "but I can only do it once."

I conferred with Howie and Ira about it, because I felt I had no one else to talk to.

"Maybe he'll paint himself green and run through the school," says Ira.

"Naked!" says Howie.

"Naah," I said. "If the cat suit and the orange sombrero didn't get him noticed, no amount of green paint would."

"Maybe he's gonna skydive right into the middle of a Jets game," says Ira.

"Naked!" says Howie.

"Naah," I said. "People might remember that it happened, but they wouldn't remember it was him."

They were no help, and so, for the Schwa's sake, I put aside my own feelings of awkwardness and brought my worries to Lexie, because I knew, in spite of everything, she cared about him as much as I did.

It seemed a kind of poetic justice, or maybe just pathetic justice, that Lexie's and my relationship now revolved entirely around the Schwa.

"He won't disappear," Lexie said, after I told her the story about his mother. "He won't because *she* didn't."

"How do you know?"

"Because people just don't pop out of existence."

"Maybe they do," I said. "Maybe they do all the time, and no one notices."

That's when Crawley rolled into the room. "You're talking about our friend Mr. Schwa, aren't you."

"Since when was the Schwa your friend?" I asked.

"I was speaking figuratively."

"You should be an expert on being invisible, Grandpa," Lexie said, a little more biting than she usually was. "With all the years you've been cooped up in here."

Since nasty looks didn't work on Lexie, he gave me one instead.

"Out of sight, but not out of mind." He wheeled over to the window. I had opened one of the curtains to let some late afternoon light in, but now he tugged the curtain closed, then turned to me. "How many years have you been hearing stories about crazy Old Man Crawley?"

"For as long as I can remember," I said. "And then some."

"There, you see? There's a difference between being invisible, and being *unseen*. No one passes this restaurant without looking at these windows and wondering about me."

"So what do you think about the Schwa's mother?" I asked him. "Which is she, invisible or unseen?"

"Frankly, I couldn't care less." Crawley twirled his wheelchair around and headed for the kitchen. "But, if I did care, I'm sure there would be a way to find out."

Around the corner from me lived a guy who worked for the Department of Water and Power, and he claimed to be a dowser. You've probably heard of people like this—they use wishbone-shaped twigs to tune into "earth energies" or something, and can find water underground. Anyway, this guy's name was Ed Neebly, and his job was to look for leaks in the city's water grid. I don't know if the Department of Water and Power knew he did his job by dowsing rather than by using the more traditional method, commonly called guessing.

I saw him work once in a neighbor's yard, armed with two L-shaped stainless-steel rods instead of a wishbone twig. I guess this was advanced technology for dowsers. With one rod in each hand, he paced back and forth across the yard. Neebly said that when the rods stayed parallel, it meant there was no underground leak. If the rods crossed, then there was water. Walking back and forth across the lawn, he accurately predicted where the leak in the pipe was, and everyone watching was amazed. Of course, he had been standing in a mud puddle when he made the prediction, but he claimed that was just a coincidence. I was willing to give him the benefit of the doubt.

Crawley had suggested there were ways to find out about the Schwa's mother and her vanishing act. Well, the Schwa was convinced it was supernatural, and I wasn't going to deny the possibility that maybe he was right. Maybe she had a terminal case of the Schwa Effect, and when no one was looking the universe kind of just swallowed her without as much as a burp. Then again, though, maybe there *was* a burp—and that's where Ed Neebly came in. According to *Ripley's Believe It or Not*, any halfway decent dowser could also go dowsing for spirits and other "paranormal phenomena." It's one of those do-not-try-this-at-home kind of things, because if you're like me, you really don't want to know how many people died in your bedroom.

"I do believe in auras and energy fields," Lexie told me, "but I don't know if I believe in this."

Still, we hired Neebly to bring his dowsing talents to the Waldbaum's in Canarsie—the alleged supermarket where the Schwa's alleged mother allegedly vanished. He didn't charge us anything. "Consider it a community service," Neebly told us. "When we're done, pay me what you think it's worth."

For this task, his dowsing rods were made of glass. "Glass resonates with the spirit world more than metal," Neebly said. "Spirits find metal irritating and head the other way. True."

Lexie, Moxie, and I followed him as he wove up and down the aisles of Waldbaum's like we were some goofy Scooby-Doo ghost hunting squad. I tried to ignore the strange looks of the locals, but it wasn't easy.

"I feel like an idiot," I said.

"You get used to it," Neebly told me. He led us through the fruits and vegetables, hesitating for a moment by the potatoes before moving on. He thought he found some ectoplasmic slime in the condiment aisle, but it turned out to be relish.

"I've dowsed for spirits lots of times," he told us. "It's much more delicate than dowsing for water. Water always flows to the lowest point—not so with spirits!"

He stopped toward the back of the store, and his rods crossed. "There's a cold spot here."

"We're in front of the dairy case," I pointed out.

"Hmm. Could be that. Could be astral."

The look on Lexie's face was the blind version of an eyeball roll.

We purposely hadn't told Neebly where the disappearance had taken place, to see if he found it for himself. We watched him closely as he moved down the frozen-foods aisle and rounded the corner, toward the meat counter. The rods did not cross.

"I got called out to Jersey a few months ago," he told us as he passed the chicken, then the pork, then the beef. "A woman had a poltergeist living in her duplex. My rods went crazy when I got to the basement." He passed the lamb and the seafood. The butcher behind the counter looked away, probably embarrassed for us. "It turns out the Mob had killed a guy and dumped him in the concrete when they poured the foundation. True." By now he had passed the butcher's counter and was headed toward the beer case, where he paused thoughtfully, although I don't think that was because of any supernatural influences.

In the end, he found no spiritual vortexes, although he did detect three leaks in the supermarket's plumbing.

We gave the supernatural angle a rest, but returned the next day and asked to speak to the manager, who said he had worked there for twelve years.

"We're doing a report," I told him, "on the history of Waldbaum's."

He was thrilled to discuss it with us, telling us how Izzy Waldbaum had come over penniless from Russia a hundred years ago and opened a small bread-and-butter store on DeKalb Avenue. I'm sure it was all fascinating to someone who cared.

"We're not interested in the whole grocery-store chain," Lexie told him. "We just want to know about this store."

Before he could launch into a presentation about the opening-day ribbon-cutting ceremony, I said, "We're looking for newsworthy events that have happened since you've worked here."

Suddenly he got a caged look on his face, like corporate executives get in a *60 Minutes* interview. "Why?" he asked. "What have you heard?"

"Nothing specific," Lexie said, trying not to tip him off about the real reason for our visit. If he knew we were actually performing an investigation, he'd probably tell us to talk to their lawyers, and that would be the kiss of death. "Has the store had any robberies?"

He laughed. "Yeah, like every second Tuesday. That's not news."

"How about murders?" I asked.

"Not since I've been here."

"What about kidnappings?" Lexie said.

"Or unexplained disappearances?" I added.

"No," he said, then thought for a minute. "A kid got abandoned here once, though."

Bingo. "Abandoned?" I said, trying to stay calm. "What happened?"

"I was working produce then. From my recollection, the mother just left him in the shopping cart. Jeez—I haven't thought about that in years."

"Did they ever find the mother?" Lexie asked.

He shook his head. "I don't know. Eventually the father showed up for him."

"How about the security video?" I asked. "Did it show her leaving the store?"

"Half the cameras in the store were broken, including the one at the front door." According to the manager, the camera in the meat section worked, but it was permanently stuck in the wrong position, monitoring a sign that detailed the proper handling of pork instead of the meat counter. The only thing the police were ever able to determine was that the pork sign had not been stolen.

"Come to think of it, they fired the manager over the broken video cameras. That's when I got bumped up to assistant manager, and then manager a couple of years later." He smiled, reliving the memory.

"So, theoretically," I said, "she may never have left the store."

He laughed. "Yeah, who knows? Maybe she ended up as hamburger." Then his eyes got all darty and nervous again. "You're not gonna quote me on that, are you?"

Even though it was hard to keep the Schwa in my mind, our investigations kept me thinking about his parents a lot. What was it that made a mother disappear between the lines of her shopping list? And what made a father remove every trace of her from the house? I would look at my own father and wonder if there were moments when he forgot I existed, too. I would look at my mom and wonder about her trips to the market.

At least now we had confirmation that something did actually happen to the Schwa's mom, although there was still no telling what. When I got home later that afternoon, just Mom and Christina were there. Mom was cooking something called coq au vin in a big frying pan. It was French, and smelled really good. She claimed it had no ingredients we wouldn't eat by themselves, and she had me taste a spoonful of the sauce. It got my mouth watering. As I watched her cook, I thought about the Schwa's mother, a woman so unnoticed she could walk into a supermarket, not walk out again, and no one would notice. My mom was anything but invisible, but maybe she didn't know it.

"If you're gonna stand there, then make yourself useful." She handed me a strainer and poured some boiling string beans through it.

"Mom, I just want you to know . . . that I know how hard you work."

She looked at me like I might have a fever. "Thank you, Anthony. It's good to hear that from you."

"Just promise me you're never gonna disappear, okay?"

She chuckled. "Okay, sure. I'll stay far away from David Copperfield."

She returned to her food, and I put the string beans in a serving bowl.

"So, you like the cooking class?"

"Love it."

"And you're not mad at Dad anymore?"

She stirred her simmering sauce a bit. "I wasn't really mad at him." She added chicken pieces to the pan—enough to feed the whole family. "I always knew your father was a better cook than me. But this kitchen was my place. I know it's old-fashioned, but I chose it. Your aunt Mona, I don't think she ever cooked a meal in her life. She wanted a career. Good for her—I've got no problem with that. But sometimes you get a career and then you suddenly realize you don't have a life. Or if you stay at home with your family, you suddenly realize that your life is actually everyone else's life, not your own. Either way, when you got all your eggs in one basket, the basket gets heavy. Maybe the eggs start to break."

"So get yourself a few more baskets," I said. "Spread 'em out." And then I realized that's exactly what she was doing. That's why she was taking classes. That's why she was getting a job. It was all about spreading out those eggs. She had to feel she had a place in her own life, or else maybe she thought she'd disappear somehow, too. Maybe not all at once like the Schwa's mom, but a little bit every day.

The changes she was making scared me a little, though. I

guess because I knew she'd be meeting new people, and I wondered if maybe those new people might be more interesting than the Vice-Vice-President of Product Development for Pisher Plastics.

"So how about the first basket?" I asked. "You think that first basket that held the eggs will be okay? I mean, you wouldn't throw it away, right?"

She chuckled again. "When have you ever known me to throw anything away?"

I hugged her. It had been such a long time since I had really hugged her, it felt weird. Used to be I would disappear into her when she hugged me; now it was almost the other way around.

"You're a good boy, Anthony," she told me. "No matter what anybody says."

A Late-Night Trip to the Land
of Beef That Could Turn a Person
into a Vegetarian

16 The Schwa was fading, no question about it, and it started to hit me that maybe he was right. Maybe he would sift deeper and deeper through everyone's mind until he just dropped right out the bottom and vanished completely. I noticed him less and less in class, and when it did occur to me to look for him, I always freaked out until I located him in the classroom. It kept getting harder to remind myself to remember him. It's like my mind was a sieve, and not its usual sieve, because there were some things I was very good at remembering, like faces, or names, or sports stats. But the Schwa, he was like history. He was like trying to remember Lewis and Clark, and Manifest Destiny—both of which I had to do oral reports on, and if you've ever had to do an oral report, you probably know how they make you dress up like whoever you're doing the report on, but how was I supposed to dress up like Manifest Destiny? I got marked down because I wore jeans and a T-shirt—even though I argued that Levi Strauss was making jeans during the westward expansion, and that's why they call them Levi's—but what was I talking about? Oh, right. So now I had to wonder whether some kind of destiny was manifesting itself on the Schwa.

It had been a week since Lexie and I had set out on our less-than-successful attempt to track down what really happened to his mother. The Schwa still hadn't given me any hints as to what ammunition he was going to use in his one-man war to un-Schwa himself and be noticed in a major way. I was worried about him. Really worried.

It was Tuesday. Crawley was between nurses—they never lasted in his company for more than a few days. It had become a game with him to see how quickly he could send them packing. A new, unsuspecting home-care victim was due that night, but since Lexie had an afternoon meeting of the 4-S Club, I figured I'd hang out with Crawley after I walked the dogs so he wouldn't be alone. I brought him over some stuffed focaccia my dad made to go with Mom's veau Marseille last night.

As I brought back the last of the dogs, I caught him in a rare moment. He was petting Charity, and talking to her gently, lovingly saying all those sweet, stupid things we say to pets when we think no one's looking. He caught me watching him and abruptly stopped.

"Don't you have some dogs to walk?"

"All done."

"Then why are you still here? It's not payday."

I shrugged. "I thought I'd wait until the new nurse got here. Maybe eat some of my dad's focaccia."

"It's gone."

"You ate it all?"

"It was too good for you anyway," he said. "You'd just wolf it down without tasting it."

"Maybe we should call you Gluttony," I said. At that, Gluttony came over to me, hope in his eyes.

He laughed. "Now he's *your* problem."

I decided to take a chance. I had seen a moment of tenderness rise to the surface a few moments ago. I thought that maybe I might be able to ask Crawley something and actually get a thoughtful answer.

"Do you remember him?" I asked.

"Remember who?"

"The Schwa."

"Why would I want to?"

"Because," I told him, "I really think he's starting to disappear."

Crawley just stared at me coldly. I sighed.

"Forget it," I said. "You probably think I'm an idiot."

"That's beside the point," he said. Then he stood up out of his wheelchair and grabbed a cane that was leaning against the wall. I had never seen him get up from his wheelchair before. It was like watching one of those faith healings. Crawley strode toward me slowly, holding the cane tightly. He was taller than I realized. He took about five or six steps, then stopped right in front of me.

"I don't recall his face," Crawley said. "But I do remember him being here."

He took one more step, and then had me help him sit on the sofa.

"I didn't know you could walk."

"As I said when you so rudely broke into my home two

months ago, the wheelchair is only temporary." He got himself comfortable on the sofa, and I sat in the plush chair across from him.

"I'm sure you think it's a miracle that I can walk," he said. "Well, I believe we make our own miracles." He leaned his cane gently against the edge of the sofa. "I also believe we make our own disasters. If your friend is disappearing, as you say, then he's doing it to himself."

A pack of Afghans frolicked past, knocking down the cane. I picked it up and gave it to him again. "He's trying not to. He's trying to be visible."

"Then he's not trying the right way. The universe has no sympathy, and we're never rewarded for doing things the improper way." Prudence came over for attention, and Crawley began to scratch her behind the neck. "If your friend continues on his path of self-destructive anonymity, you should minimize your own losses. Cut him loose. Forget about him."

"He's my friend."

"Spare me your sentimentality," said Crawley. "Friends can be replaced."

"No, they can't!"

Instead of answering me right away, he looked down at the dog, which was so utterly content to have a fraction of his attention. "Four years ago," he said, "Prudence was hit by a car and killed."

He said it so bluntly, the news actually made me gasp.

"So," he continued, "I fired my dog walker, and I contacted a breeder. Prudence was replaced within three weeks, and life went on. As I said, friends can be replaced."

I was so horrified by this, I couldn't say a thing.

"All of my dogs are second generation," he told me. "Some even third. All sins, all virtues. It's the way I like it."

"That's wrong," I said. It was twisted in some basic way—like those people who have their pets stuffed and stick them in front of the fireplace like a piece of furniture. They don't even have real eyes anymore. How could you stand looking at a stuffed pet with marbles for eyes? And how could you treat pets and people like objects to be replaced? "More than wrong—it's kind of sick."

"Think what you want, but it's the way the world works."

"What do you know about the world? You're not a part of it—you live outside of it, in your own weird little universe."

He grabbed his cane, reached across the table, and poked me in the chest. "You're nervy," he said. "I used to like that about you, but now it's rubbing me the wrong way."

I stood up. Suddenly I didn't feel like being in the same room with him. I didn't feel like being on the same continent. "Now I know why you're so afraid of dying," I told him just before I left. "Because you know when the time comes, you won't be rewarded for living your life 'the improper way.'"

As I left, I thought about Lexie's plan to traumatize him for his own good, and took a twisted kind of pleasure knowing that some sort of suffering was in store for him. I had a suspicion, though, that Crawley would be a hard egg to crack.

I knew I wasn't going to sleep much that night, so I didn't even try. If the Schwa Effect was hereditary, then the key to everything was finding out what happened to his mom. The thing is, if the whole problem revolved around not being noticed, how could we find an eyewitness? If the Schwa Effect led to being universally forgotten, how could I hope that anyone would remember?

Our little dowsing session with Ed Neebly and our conversation with the supermarket manager had been about as helpful as a New Jersey road sign, and if you've ever been there, you know the signs don't tell you the exit you're coming up to, they only point out the exits you've just missed. It puts parents in very foul moods—and since you're probably there to visit relatives, their mood was pretty touch and go to begin with. As for my own parents, I'm sure they would have blown a gasket if they knew what I was about to do.

I had never been the kind of kid to sneak out late at night. I was more the kind of guy who would come home ridiculously late and suffer the consequences, but once I was home for the night, sneaking out was never an option. I've got this screen saver that I don't use very much, on account of how lame it is. It's a cartoon of a computer wearing a nightcap and snoring. But if you darken the screen so no one can see the picture, and you set the volume just right, you'd swear there was a real person sleeping in the room. The pillows I had shoved under my blanket weren't very convincing, but add the snoring from my computer and suddenly it was like I had a roommate. I quietly slipped out, to catch a bus toward Canarsie.

The butcher had looked away.

At the time I was so involved with what Ed Neebly was doing I didn't think much of it, but my mind kept coming back to that moment. The butcher hadn't just turned to look at something else, he had purposely avoided my gaze. He knew something. The chances of me finding him at this hour of the night were slim, but then I wouldn't have much luck during the day either, because of the manager. The manager had gotten so paranoid by the end of our questioning that he sent all the stock clerks to get rid of expired dairy products, in case we were taking notes for some major exposé. He had banned Lexie and me from the store—even though Lexie threatened to sic the 4-S Club after him.

Waldbaum's was a twenty-four-hour supermarket, I guess so if you had a sudden need for hair gel or Häagen-Dazs at three in the morning, relief was only minutes away. That also meant that I could avoid the manager during the off-hours—and chances were, if the butcher knew something about the Schwa's mother, other people who worked there knew something, too.

It was almost midnight by the time I got there. I walked down the frozen-food aisle and turned left, heading toward the meat department. The little counter where the butcher took custom orders was unlit—but that didn't necessarily mean no one was there. Supermarkets had whole back areas like they've got at airports, where employees hang out, rummaging through lost luggage and stuff. Not that lost luggage would be in a supermarket, but considering how airlines work, it wouldn't surprise me to find socks from yesterday's flight to Cleveland in with the veal chops.

In the dark display case, the unpackaged meat was arranged like perfect works of art. Pork chops were layered in a left-right alternating pattern. Rib-eye steaks were neatly pushed together like interlocking floor tiles. Someone had taken great care with this meat. It was weird to think that a butcher would care enough to be so particular. When you think about it, being a butcher has got to be one of the most unpleasant jobs in the world, except for maybe those ladies who cut toenails. I mean, who'd want to spend all day chopping and grinding animals into little pieces? But then, on the other hand, it probably gives guys that would otherwise be ax murderers a healthy outlet. As it turned out, this theory was about to be proven.

I heard a noise coming from one of those "employee-only" back rooms. It was a high-pitched whine, like a vacuum sucking helium. I followed that sound through a pair of floppy double doors and found myself in a white tile and stainless-steel room, full of meat-cutting equipment. The place had an unfriendly fermented smell, like an old refrigerator crossed with my brother Frankie's feet. A guy in goggles and a stained white smock stood at the far end of the room at a stainless-steel table, cutting up a side of beef with what looked like a band saw. He did it with such concentration, you'd think it was brain surgery.

This was the last guy in the world you'd want to see near a sharp object. He was tall but hunched, his neck sticking forward at an angle that made my own neck hurt just watching him. His hair was thin and unkempt. I couldn't tell if it was white or just very, very blond. I could see patches of red scalp through his hair.

"Excuse me," I said, but he didn't hear me. He just kept on cutting the meat. The machine let off a grating whine whenever it hit the bone.

"Excuse me," I said again, a bit louder this time.

Without looking at me, he turned off the saw, and it buzzed itself silent. "You are not supposed to be here!"

He had a strange accent. Almost German, but not quite.

"I just want to ask you a few questions. You're the butcher here, right?"

"I am the night butcher," he said.

Okay, now here's the part of the movie where a kid with any brains gets out of there, unless he wants to end up in neatly arranged portions in the display case, because no kid with any brains is gonna stand alone in a room full of knives, saws, and grinders with anyone who calls himself the "Night Butcher."

"You come to taunt me more, eh?" he said, raising his voice. "You and your friends. *Letting the air out of my tires, scribbling rude words on my windows. This I know! You think I don't?"*

"I can see it's not a good time. I'll come back tomorrow."

I backed up, but missed the door and knocked over a broom. The handle hit the floor with a nasty *thwok,* and my heart ran to hide somewhere in my left shoe.

"No!" he said. "You have business with me, you tell me now. We settle this here!"

He came toward me. I could see that his neck was scaly, and red as raw meat.

"We have nothing to settle," I told him. "I didn't let the air out of your tires, or anything. Trust me, I've got better things to do than mess with the Night Butcher."

He scratched his neck thoughtfully. "And I should believe you?"

"Yeah."

He took off his goggles to get a better look at me. His eyes were as wild as his hair. Then he said, "I believe you. For now. What is it you want?"

"I'm trying to help a friend," I said. "How long have you worked for Waldbaum's?"

"Flemish!" he shouted.

"Huh?"

"You are wondering about my accent. It is Flemish. I come from Belgium. All you know from Belgium is waffles and chocolate. Now you know me."

"Great, got it—waffles, chocolate, and you. So how long have you worked for Waldbaum's?"

"Nineteen years. I was here when cuts were thick, and you could still get a lamb chop with a nice big fillet, back when meat was meat." He looked off for a moment, nostalgic for the good old days, then said, "Gunther!"

"Huh?"

"You are wondering what is my name."

"Well, not really, but thanks for telling me." This was the only human being I'd ever met who had more trouble than me staying on the subject. "Did you always work in this store, or did you get moved around?"

"Always here," he said.

"Good. So you were here about nine years ago when a little boy got left in a shopping cart."

Suddenly his whole attitude changed. "No." He turned back to the beef he had been cutting. "I was not on duty yet. I do not remember."

"If you don't remember, how could you know you weren't on duty?"

He scratched his peeling neck. Little flakes fell to the cutting table. I'm never eating meat from Waldbaum's again.

"Eczema," he said.

"Huh?"

"You are wondering about my neck. Why I scratch."

"What you do with your neck is your business."

He stopped scratching and looked at me for an uncomfortably long time. "You are this little boy from the shopping cart?" he asked.

"No, but I'm his friend."

Gunther nodded, then went to remove his smock and washed his hands. "This friend of yours. He is okay now?"

"Not really," I told him. I thought of what story I could make up to get Gunther to spill his guts, and then I figured the truth would do the job just fine. "He thinks his mother disappeared into thin air, and he never got over it."

Gunther sighed. "I am very sorry to hear that." He pulled up a chair and sat down, then pulled up one for me. "Sit."

Although I really didn't want to, I knew I might finally be onto something. I sat down, and Gunther took his time before he spoke again.

"You have to understand, this was none of my business. I had nothing to do with it, I only saw."

Bingo! "So you saw what happened! She didn't disappear after all, did she?"

Gunther sighed. "She did disappear, in a manner of speaking," he said. "And she was not the only one who disappeared that night."

I waited for more, but then he sat back, thought for a moment, and said, "No." He stood and returned to his meat cutting.

"What do you mean 'no'? You can't start and not finish."

He slammed the side of beef back down on the cutting table. "I tell this story only once. Your friend should be here when I do. Bring your friend and I will tell you both about that day."

Then he gave me four pork chops, cut thick like they used to in the days when meat was meat, and he sent me on my way.

A Traumatic Experience I'll Live to Regret, Assuming I Live

17 Just as she had promised, Lexie sprung a top-secret trauma attack on her grandfather. It came without warning (without me being warned, that is) the morning after my visit to the Night Butcher. It was Saturday. A day I should have been able to sleep late. As I was tossing and turning all night with unpleasant dreams about meat, I was dead to the world when the phone rang. My mom practically had to use heart paddles to wake me up.

"She says it's important," my mom said, shoving the phone into my hand. "I don't know what could be so important at seven in the morning."

"Hewwo?" I said, sounding more like Elmer Fudd than I truly want to admit.

"Today's the day," Lexie said excitedly on the end of the line. "Everything's set for noon."

"Huh? What everything do you mean?" I croaked out.

"Trauma therapy," she whispered. "My grandfather—remember?"

I groaned, and Lexie got all annoyed.

"Well, if you don't want to help, you don't have to come. It's not like you're under any obligation."

"No, no," I said. "I want to help," which was true. Traumatizing Old Man Crawley was actually pretty high on my list of Things I'd Most Like to Do. "What do you need me to bring?"

"Just yourself," she said, "And Calvin. Tell him I want him to come, too."

"Why don't *you* tell him?"

Lexie hesitated. "I haven't spoken to him since the day we all broke up."

After Lexie hung up, I dialed the Schwa. It rang once, and I hung up. My encounter with the Night Butcher was still fresh in my mind, and I knew if I talked to him, he'd hear something funny in my voice. I wanted to tell him about it, but a sensitive matter like this had to be handled carefully, at the right time and place.

The phone rang, and figuring it was Lexie again, I picked it right up.

"Hi, Antsy, it's Calvin."

"Schwa?" He caught me completely off guard.

"Yeah. You rang a second ago. So what's up?"

He had star-sixty-nined me. Curse telephone technology. "Uh . . . so whatcha up to today?"

"I've got big plans," he said. "The biggest! Of course I can't tell you about it just yet."

He was so excited, I knew he was itching to talk about it as much as he wanted to keep it a secret. I should have asked him about it. That's what friends do, right? They nag you until you tell them the secret they're pretending they don't want to tell. The Schwa needed that kind of friend now; one who would listen, and yell at him, "What, are you insane?" And maybe stop him from doing something he'd regret. I should have been that kind of friend.

"Cool," I said. "Guess I'll see you on Monday." And I hung up. I didn't ask him what he was planning, I didn't tell him about the Night Butcher, and I didn't invite him to traumatize Crawley with us. You never realize when you make little choices how big those choices can be. I can't really be held responsible for everything that happened next, but if I had made the right decision, things could have turned out differently.

At noon I stood at Crawley's door, taking a few deep breaths. Some dogs were already barking on the other side, sensing me there. One more breath and I pounded on the door over and over, until all the dogs were barking.

"Mr. Crawley! Mr. Crawley! Hurry, open up!"

I heard him cursing at the dogs, a few dead bolts slid, and the door cracked open just enough to reveal four chains stretched like iron cobwebs between me and Crawley's scowling face.

"What? What is it?"

"It's Lexie! She fell down the stairs. I think she broke something. Maybe a few things."

"I'll call 911."

"No! No, she's asking for you—you've gotta come!"

He hesitated for a moment. The door closed, I heard the chains sliding open, and he pulled the door open again. Prudence and a few of the other dogs got out, but Crawley didn't seem to care. He just stood there at the door.

"Mr. Crawley, come on!"

The look of fear on his face was like someone standing on the edge of a cliff instead of someone on the threshold of an apartment. "Aren't there people helping her?"

"Yeah, but she's asking for you."

As if on cue, Lexie wailed from the bottom of the stairs.

"Mr. Crawley—she's your granddaughter! Are you just going to stand there?"

He took the first step, and it seemed the next ones were a little bit easier. Then, when he got to the top of the stairs and saw *her sprawled at the very bottom, he flew to her side like a man* half his age.

"Lexie, honey—it'll be okay. Tell me where it hurts." He looked at the gawking waiters and diners. "Didn't any of you morons call an ambulance?"

And with that, Lexie stood up. I grabbed Crawley's left arm, Lexie's harmonica-playing driver grabbed his right, and we whisked him through the kitchen and out the restaurant's back door before anyone knew what was happening.

It was a nasty trick, but there weren't many things that would get Crawley down those stairs. Lexie had the easy part—lying there pretending to be hurt, but I was the one who had to get him to come out. I'm not much of an actor. In grade school, I usually got roles like "Third Boy, " or "Middle Broccoli," or in one embarrassing year, "Rear End of Horse." I had no confidence in my ability to pull this off, but the fact that I was so nervous had actually helped.

By the time Crawley gathered up enough of his wits to realize this was a conspiracy, we already had him in the backseat of the Lincoln. When he tried to escape, I got in his way and closed the door—which was protected by child locks so it couldn't be opened from the inside.

I won't repeat the words Crawley shouted at us. Some of them were words I didn't even know—and I know quite a lot.

"You're not getting out of this," I told him, "so you might as well cooperate."

He turned to Lexie. "What is this all about? Did *he* put you up to this?"

"It's my idea, Grandpa."

"This is kidnapping!" he squealed. "I'll press charges."

"I can just see the headlines," Lexie said.

"Yeah," I added. "'Rich Kook Presses Charges on Poor Blind Granddaughter.' The press will eat it up."

"You shut up!" he said. "By the time you get out of jail, you'll have gray hair."

"Naah," I said. "I'll be bald, more likely. It runs in my family."

The fact that I didn't seem to care made him even more furious.

By the time we pulled out of the alley we had put a blindfold on him, and he didn't resist because he didn't want to see the outside world anyway. He was quiet for a minute, then he said, "What are you going to do to me?" He was truly frightened now. I almost felt sorry for him. The key word here is "almost."

"I have no idea," I told him, which was true—Lexie still hadn't told me what she had planned. She said I'd chicken out if I knew, and so I didn't press her, figuring she might be right. We rode to Brooklyn Heights—the part of Brooklyn that faced Manhattan right across the East River. Then we drove onto a pier. That's when I figured out what Lexie had planned.

"Oh, wow," I said. "You've got to be kidding!"

"What!" shouted Crawley. "Kidding about what? What is it?" But he made no attempt to uncover his eyes.

"You can't be serious," I told Lexie. "It'll kill him."

The driver opened the door. "Sorry about this, Mr. Crawley," said the driver in a heavy accent. "But Lexie say this for your own good."

"Is it a boat?" Crawley asked, obviously smelling the stench of the river. "I hate boats!"

"No boat," said the driver. He helped Lexie out. "Leave me hold Moxie. You go."

No one, not even the driver, was willing to tell Crawley that his next mode of transportation was going to be a helicopter. He'd have to discover that for himself.

I led him down the pier to the heliport at the very end, and he didn't fight me. He was broken now. Too scared to run, too scared to do anything but go where we led him. He stumbled a few times on the weed-cracked pavement, but I had a good hold on him. I wasn't going to let him fall. "Big step up," I told him.

"Up to where?"

I gave him no answer, but once he was seated and I had strapped him in, I think he figured it out.

He moaned the deep moan of the condemned. The pilot, who I guess was hired by Lexie for our little therapeutic flight, waited until we were all strapped in. Then he started the engine. Crawley whimpered. Okay, now I really did feel sorry for him. Lexie just said, "This is going to be fun, Grandpa."

"You terrible, terrible girl."

I began to wonder if Lexie had gone too far. She did tend to have a blind spot for others' feelings, and that was one place Moxie couldn't guide her. The helicopter powered up, the slow *foom-foom-foom* of the blades speeding into a steady whir. We wobbled for an instant, then went straight up, like an elevator with no cable. Through the large window I saw the strange sight of Lexie's driver holding on to Moxie and waving good-bye.

"You can take off your blindfold now, Grandpa."

"No, I won't!" he said, like a child. "You can't make me." He clapped his hands tightly over his eyes, keeping the blindfold firmly in place.

I had only been in an airplane to Disney World and back—and both times it was at night, so I didn't get to see much. This flight wasn't for my benefit, but still it sucked my breath right out of my chest—and I don't think it was just the altitude. *The Schwa would have loved this,* I thought, then I pushed the thought away. Thinking of him now would only bring me down, and I didn't want to be brought down.

We flew along the East River, Brooklyn to our right, the skyscrapers of Manhattan to our left. All the while the old man groaned and refused to take his hands from his eyes.

"Anthony," yelled Lexie, over the beating of the blades. "Can you describe it to me?"

"Sure."

"Don't use sight words."

By now I'd become good at describing things for four senses instead of five. "Okay. We're flying right over the Brooklyn Bridge. It's a harp strung across the river, with a frame made of rough stone."

The pilot took a left turn, and brought us right into the city.

"What else?" prompted Lexie.

"We're passing downtown now. There's uh, . . . the Wool-worth Building, I think. It's roof is a cold metal pyramid with a sharp point, but the sun's hitting it, making it hot. Moving toward midtown now. There's Broadway. It kind of slices a weird angle through all the rest of the streets, and there's traffic jams where it hits all the other avenues. There's little bumps of taxis everywhere, like hundreds of lemon candies filling the streets. You could read the streets like Braille."

"Ooh, that's good!" Lexie said.

I was on a roll. "Uh . . . Grand Central Station ahead of us. Like a Greek temple—lots of pillars and sculptures sticking out of the dry, musty old stonework. And above it, smack in the middle of Park Avenue, like it shouldn't even be there, is the MetLife Building. This big old cheese grater, like eighty stories high."

And then Crawley said "Used to be the Pan Am Building. Pan Am. Now there was a company!"

Lexie smiled, and I finally understood. The descriptions weren't for Lexie—they were for her grandfather. "Keep going, Anthony." Crawley's hands were still over his face, but they weren't pressed as tightly as before. I continued, but now I was talking to Crawley instead of to Lexie.

"The Chrysler Building. Sharp. Icy. The highest point of a Christmas tree star. Okay, the heart of midtown coming up. Rockefeller Center, smooth old granite, in the middle of all these steel-and-glass skyscrapers. Trump Tower. It's like a jagged crystal that got shoved out of the ground."

That did it. Crawley took his hands from his eyes, slipped off the blindfold, and took in the view.

"Oh . . . !" was all he could say. He gripped his seat, like it might accidentally eject him, and he just stared at everything we passed. We flew over Central Park, then over the West Side, and headed downtown again, over the Hudson River.

Through all of this, Crawley said nothing. His face was pale, his lips were pursed. I thought for sure that he was completely lost in a state of shock, never to shout a foul word again, just staring forever, his mind an absolute blank.

We took a trip around the Statue of Liberty, and then we came back to where we started. The helicopter dropped us off on the pier, where Lexie's driver was waiting, playing his harmonica. When we were safe in the Lincoln and on our way home, Crawley finally spoke.

"You will never be forgiven for this," he said. "Neither of you. And you will pay."

We rode the rest of the way in silence.

Larger Than Life, in Your Face, Undeniable Schwa

18 I had made up my mind to tell the Schwa about the Night Butcher the very next day, but he was nowhere to be found. His father was no help—he suggested that he might be at school, and was once more baffled when I told him it was Sunday.

It was late that afternoon that my dad came to get me in my room. "Hey, Antsy, that kid is here," he says. "The one who makes your mother nervous." I knew exactly who he was talking about. We had him over for dinner once, and the Schwa rubbed my mom the wrong way. First because he ate his pasta plain—no sauce, no butter, nothing. That alone made him a suspicious character. Then my mom kept whacking him in the face. Not because she meant to, but he always seemed to be standing right there, where she wasn't expecting, and she talks with her hands.

"What are you doing right now?" the Schwa asked the second he saw me.

"The usual," I said.

"Good. I've got something to show you."

Right away I knew this was it. The visibility play.

"How long will it take?" I asked, "because I gotta go walk the sins and virtues . . . and besides, I've got something important to talk to you about, too."

"Not long," he said. "Go get your bus pass." And then he added. "You're going to love this!"

But I wasn't so sure.

That chilly afternoon, we took a bus past Bensonhurst, past Bay Ridge, past all the civilized sections of Brooklyn, to a place they would have called the Edge of the Earth in the days before Columbus. This was an old part of Brooklyn, where the shore curved back toward Manhattan. It was full of docks that hadn't been used since before my parents were born, and old warehouses ten stories high, with windows that were all broken, boarded up, or covered with fifty years of New York grime. People pass by this place all the time but never stop, because they're on the Gowanus Expressway—the elevated highway that cuts right through this dead place. There's a street that runs right underneath the elevated road. I figured it would be just as abandoned as the rest of the area, but today there was traffic like you couldn't believe.

"Could you tell me what we're doing here?" I asked him on the bus ride.

"Nope." The Schwa was as serious as I'd ever seen him. "You'll have to wait and see."

The bus made only three intersections in twenty minutes,

riding beneath the girders that held up the expressway. Frustrated drivers leaned on their horns, like the gridlock was the fault of the person in front of them.

The Schwa stood up and looked out of the window. "C'mon, we'll walk."

"Are you kidding me? The people around here look like extras from *Night of the Living Dead*—and those are just the people on the bus!" Across the aisle, a living-dead guy gave me a dirty look.

"If you're worried," the Schwa said, "hide behind me. They won't notice you if you're behind me."

It was half past four in the afternoon when we got off the bus. It was already getting dark, and I was quaking at the thought of having to wait for a bus back from this rank corner of the world. I hoped the street ahead stayed crowded with cars so at least our bodies would be recovered quickly.

We walked for four blocks underneath the Gowanus Expressway, passing identical warehouses, all of which had been condemned by the city, with big signs, like it was something the city was proud of. Then the Schwa went to one of the warehouse entrances and pushed open a door that almost snapped off its rusted hinges.

"In there?" I asked. "What's in there?"

"You'll see."

"You're annoying."

"Not for much longer."

I stepped in, against my survival instinct. The building was no warmer than the street outside, and it smelled like something died in there from smelling something else that died in there. That mixed with some weird solvent fumes made me gag.

I heard the scurry of rats, which I hoped were cats, and the flutter of bats, which I hoped were pigeons. I was just glad it was too dark to tell. The Schwa pressed a tiny flashlight on his key chain and led me up a staircase littered with wood chips and broken glass.

"The elevator doesn't work," the Schwa said. "And even if it did, I wouldn't trust it."

I tried to imagine what he could possibly be up to here, and none of it was good. I just let him lead me, hoping that I would eventually understand.

He pushed open the seventh-floor door to reveal a huge concrete expanse with nothing breaking up the space except peeling pillars holding up the ceiling above. The rot-and-solvent smell was gone, but the mustiness of the place caught in the back of my throat, making my mouth taste bitter, like juice after toothpaste.

The Schwa walked around the huge place, his arms spread wide like it was something to show off. "So what do you think?"

"I think a room just opened up for you at Bellevue's mental ward," I told him. "Do you want me to call or fax in your reservation?"

"Okay, so maybe it's not such a great place, but you can't beat the view."

He led me over to one of the broken windows. I looked out. To the left I could see the spires of Manhattan, and below was a stretch of the expressway, which ran right past the building. There were a couple of crumbling industrial streets, and past that, Greenwood Cemetery, the size of a small city itself.

"What am I supposed to see?"

The Schwa looked out of the window. The sun was already

beneath the horizon, and the twilight was quickly becoming night.

"Shh," said the Schwa. "Any second now."

Those few minutes of waiting made me worry even more. I started to babble. "Schwa, I don't know what you think you're doing here, but whatever it is, things aren't so bad, right?"

"Here it comes," he said. "Watch this."

I pulled him back from the window, afraid he might be preparing to jump, but he shook me off.

My heart was pounding a hip-hop beat in my chest as I stared out of the window. That's when the streetlights began to flicker on.

"They never come on exactly at sunset," the Schwa said. "You'd think they'd figure out that the time of sunset is different every day, but they never seem to change the streetlights until daylight savings."

More and more lights came on, then spotlights came on, lighting up the billboards overlooking the expressway. One giant billboard advertised a Spanish TV station. A second one advertised an expensive car, and a third one had a big smiling Schwa face staring out at us.

"Oh, wow!"

There was no question about it. The huge billboard was covered in Schwa. His face was the size of a hot-air balloon looming over the expressway, and next to his picture were words in red block letters:

CALVIN
SCHWA
WAS
HERE

"Oh, wow," I said again. He was right; the view from the seventh floor was wild.

"I *will* be seen," he proclaimed. "Nobody can make *that* disappear. I've rented it for a whole month!"

"It must have cost a fortune!"

"Half a fortune," he told me. "The company rented me the billboard at half the usual rate. They were really nice about it."

"It still must have been a lot."

The Schwa shrugged like it didn't matter. "My dad had money put aside for me. A college fund."

"You blew your college fund?!" I didn't like the sound of this at all, but he still acted like it didn't matter. "Weren't they suspicious about a kid renting a billboard?"

"They never knew! I did the whole thing online!" The Schwa told me how he had done it. First he set up a fake website that made it look like he ran a publicity company, then he hired an advertising agency—again online—telling them his company was promoting a new child star, Calvin Schwa. "They never questioned anything, because they got the money up front," he said. "And money talks."

I looked again at the billboard. With the streetlights on, and all the billboards lit up, the sky suddenly seemed dark. So did the expressway. In fact, the expressway seemed very dark. Then a nasty realization began to dawn on me with the slow but inescapable pain of a swift kick to Middle Earth, if you know what I mean. Something was very wrong with this picture. Not the Schwa's massive billboard picture, but the bigger picture. I swallowed hard, and my heart started hip-hopping again. I wondered how long it would take the Schwa to notice. He seemed so thrilled as he stared at his own unavoidable face, I wondered if he ever would. I thought about how you're not supposed to wake sleepwalkers, and wondered if bursting a friend's bubble was the same thing. Then I realized that I didn't want to. Let him have his dream. Let him be like his father just this once, and happily sleepwalk through this.

"It's getting late—we'd better go," I told him, trying to lure him away from that window.

"In a few minutes," he said, still marveling at the billboard. "Do you know how many thousands of people pass this spot every day?"

I tried to tug him away from the window. "Yeah, yeah. Let's just go!"

"Do you have any idea how many cars are going to drive by and—" That's where he stopped, and I knew it was all over. His bubble didn't just burst, it detonated.

"Where . . . are . . . the cars?" He said it slowly. Just like someone who really was waking up out of a dream.

"Forget it, Schwa. Let's just go."

I grabbed him and he shook me off. He stuck his whole head so far out of the broken window, I was afraid his throat would get slit on the broken glass.

He looked to the left, looked to the right, then pulled his head back in and looked at me.

"Where are all the cars, Antsy?"

I sighed. "There aren't any."

"What do you mean 'there aren't any'?"

"The Gowanus Expressway is closed for construction."

The Schwa gave me an expression so blank, I swear I really could see right through him. "Construction. . ." he echoed.

We both looked out of the window again. There were no

bright pinpoints of headlights rolling toward us, no dim red glow of taillights moving away. There were no cars on the Gowanus Expressway. Not one. It was the reason the street below the expressway was so gridlocked. It was also probably the reason those bastards had rented Schwa the billboard for half price.

"But . . . but people will see!" the Schwa insisted. "They'll see. All the buildings around here. People will look out of the buildings!"

I nodded. I didn't say what I was thinking. That this whole area was abandoned. Looking out of the window, I saw no lights in any of the other windows around us, and certainly no one looking from Greenwood Cemetery. The Schwa could see that for himself.

"Schwa, I'm sorry."

He took a deep breath, then another, then another. Then he said, "It's okay, Antsy. It's okay. Not a problem."

We went down the stairs in silence, no sounds but the shards of glass crunching beneath our feet and the impatient honks of horns coming from the traffic-packed street below the expressway. It was still bumper-to-bumper when we got out into the street.

"Bus?" I asked him.

"Later," he answered.

I followed him five blocks to a ramp that led up to the elevated roadway. It was blocked by a barricade and lined with yellow caution flashers. He squeezed through, and I went up with him.

It's weird being on a major roadway built for six lanes of traffic but carrying none. It made me feel like I was in one of those end-of-the-world movies where there's no one left but you and a bunch of evil motorcycle maniacs. I would have welcomed some motorcycle maniacs right now, to take my mind off of this billboard mess.

The Schwa doubled back in the direction we had come, walking right down the middle of the expressway. We passed in and out of little pools of light made by the billboards up above, advertising their wares to no one. Finally we reached the Schwa's billboard. This close, it loomed so much larger than life that the perspective was all off. His smile was big and fat.

He sat cross-legged in the middle of the road, looking up at himself. "It's a good picture," he said. "I smiled right. People don't always smile right when you take their picture. Usually it's fake."

"I suck at smiling," I told him. "At least when it matters." He looked at me, and I forced a lame smile, proving it.

"It cost more than just my college fund," he admitted.

"Maybe you can get your money back . . . I mean, renting you a billboard over a closed road—that's fraud."

"My fraud came first," he said. "And what goes around comes around, right?" He turned his eyes back to the billboard. "You were right, Antsy," he said. "I'm the tree."

"What?"

"The tree. The one that falls in the forest. The one that no one's there to hear."

"*I* hear you!" I told him. "*I'm* in the forest!"

"You won't be tomorrow."

I clenched my fists and growled. He was making me so angry, so frustrated. "What do you think—you're gonna wake up one morning and not exist? Are you really so crazy that you actually think that?"

He remained calm, like a monk in meditation, as he sat there cross-legged on the road. "I don't know how it will happen," he said. "Maybe I'll go to sleep and just won't be there anymore when the sun comes up. Or maybe I'll turn a corner in school and vanish into the crowd, the way my mother vanished into the crowds at the supermarket."

"Your mother!" I had almost forgotten about Gunther the butcher. I clenched my fists and kicked a clump of asphalt out of a pothole. This wasn't the time or place to talk to him about it. In his current state of mind, he wouldn't hear it anyway.

"You know, this kind of makes sense," he said. "I see that now. It didn't work because I'm not supposed to be visible. If I bought a full-page ad in the *New York Times*, there would have been a newspaper strike. If I made one of those dumb infomercials, the communications satellite would get hit by a meteor."

"What, do you think God has nothing better to do than mess with you?"

"He's all-powerful; it's not a problem for Him."

I was about to open my mouth and tell him how stupid that was, but I thought back to what Crawley had said. Although I didn't agree with the old man's jaded point of view of how the world worked, there was one thing Crawley said that had made sense. We don't get rewarded for going about things the wrong way.

"Are you just gonna sit there all night?"

"You go," he said. "I'll be all right."

"You'll get mugged."

"How could I get mugged? There's no one here."

And so he stayed there, sitting in the middle of that lonely road, staring up at his own giant face, which no one else was going to see.

He would not have moved for me alone. I was his friend, sure, but I was also the yardstick by which he measured his invisibility. I was "the control"—that's what Mr. Werthog would call me. That's the part of an experiment that's not supposed to change. It's like when you plant seeds for a science project, giving one batch plant food and a second batch Pepsi—or something bogus like that—to see if one grows better than the other. There's always a third batch you just give water so you have something to measure the other two against. The control.

No wonder the Schwa was going off the deep end—he was looking to me as the stable one.

Anyway, like I said, it would take more than me to move the Schwa from the road . . . So as soon as I left, I hunted down the closest working pay phone, dropped in some change and dialed.

"Hello, Mr. Crawley. Could you please put Lexie on?"

"If you want to talk to her, you get your irresponsible self down here and walk my dogs."

"Please. It's important."

Maybe he heard in my voice how important it was, or maybe he was just too disgusted with me to argue, but he gave Lexie the phone.

"Lexie, I need you to get your driver and meet me at the Gowanus Expressway, near the Twenty-ninth Street entrance."

"But the Gowanus Expressway is closed."

Great, I thought. She's blind, and even she knows it's closed.

How could the Schwa have missed it? "I know. I'll be waiting by the ramp. And dress warm, it's a long walk."

"To where?"

"To Calvin," I said. I guess that was the magic word.

"Okay, I'll be there as soon as I can."

As I hung up, I realized that this was the first time I had ever called him Calvin.

The Schwa Gets Radiation Therapy
in a Room That Doesn't Smell Too Good
No Matter How Much It's Disinfected

19 When he saw me approaching with Lexie, half an hour after I had left him in the road, I saw his shoulders sag.

"Why did you have to bring *her* here?" he said with nasty accusation in his eyes. "I don't feel bad enough about this already? You had to tell her, too?"

"All I told her is that you're sitting here like an idiot in the middle of road construction."

"I don't like being talked about in the third person," said Lexie.

"You chose *him*," he grumbled at her, "so why don't you both just go."

"Calvin Schwa, I am so sick of you feeling sorry for yourself," Lexie said. "Stand up."

"I'm comfortable where I am."

"I said, 'STAND UP!'"

Lexie had a pretty commanding voice. It made him leap to his feet. I jumped, too.

"We've got a car waiting," I told him. "You're coming with us, and we're not taking no for an answer."

"What am I going to do when I get home?" he asked. "What do I tell my father about the money? Can't I just stay here, close my eyes, and disappear?"

"You can't because you won't," I said. "You won't disappear, I mean. I don't know what kind of cosmic weirdness the Schwa Effect is, but it can't be terminal."

"Prove it."

"If you want proof, you have to come with us."

Lexie turned her head slightly, angling an ear to me, as if she could catch my meaning if she could hear me better. *What proof are you talking about?* her body language asked me. I didn't answer her with my voice or body, so she turned her attention back to the Schwa. Reaching toward the sound of his voice, she gently touched his face. He pulled away.

"Don't touch me if you don't mean it."

A look of hurt, maybe even insult, fell across Lexie's face. "I *always* mean it when I touch. It just may not mean what *you* think it does." She reached forward again, touching him, and this time the Schwa allowed it. Cupping his face in both of her hands, she moved her thumbs across his cold, red cheeks. It was her way of looking him in the eye.

"Antsy is not your only friend. And you have never once slipped my mind."

I could see the Schwa trying to blink away tears. I don't know exactly what he felt at that moment, but I did know that he was done with sitting in the road, feeling sorry for himself.

"Come on, Calvin," I said. "There's someplace we need to go."

"Where?"

I took a deep breath. It was time he had his own dose of trauma therapy.

"We're paying a visit to the Night Butcher."

"I'm not getting out of the car," he told me when we pulled to a stop in the parking lot of Waldbaum's supermarket.

"If you don't get out, you'll never know what happened."

"Well, *I'm* getting out," said Lexie, irritated that I had kept what little I knew from her. "Even if you don't want to hear, Calvin, I do."

In the end, he got out with us, and the three of us walked to the supermarket with the grave determination of my mother on double-coupon day.

We passed the checkers, who were complaining about the stock boys; we passed the stock boys, who were making jokes about the checkers; and we pushed our way into the room behind the meat counter without anyone noticing or caring that we were there.

Gunther was blasting the meat-cutting room with a steam hose to disinfect the stainless-steel instruments. It was a frightening noise to walk in on. A screeching hiss filled the air, which was stifling and humid. When he saw us, he stopped. He didn't yell at me this time, or make accusations. He didn't demand that we leave. He just studied us for a moment, the hose now silent in his hand.

"This is him, then? The friend?"

"This is him," I answered.

"His name is Calvin," Lexie added.

Gunther took a look at Lexie, opened his mouth as if to ask

something stupid like, "This one is blind?," but thought better of it. He put down his hose and pulled up a few chairs, the chair legs squeaking on the sweating tile floor. We all sat in silence, which was somehow worse than the awful hiss.

"You have to understand it was none of my business," Gunther began. "None of my business at all. This is why I don't speak sooner. Other people, they talk, talk, talk until words mean nothing. There is no truth." He pointed to his chest. "I keep truth here. Not in other people's ears. So you know what I say is true."

The Schwa hung on his every word, clutching the edge of his chair just like Crawley did in the helicopter. Gunther didn't speak again for a while. Maybe he wanted us to drag it out of him. Maybe he thought it was a game of twenty questions.

"Tell me what happened to my mother," the Schwa said. It turns out all Gunther was waiting for was the proper invitation—and although he claimed that his memory wasn't what it used to be, it didn't stop him from remembering things with the detail of a police report.

"The woman—your mother. She would come here all the time. Those were the days that I worked the swing shift usually. Four to midnight. Busy time. Always busy time. People rushing home from work. Dinners to make. So I always come early. Help out the day butcher. Half an hour, maybe an hour early. Your mother—I remember she came. I don't remember her face. Isn't that strange? I can't remember her face."

I looked to the Schwa to see how he would react. He didn't flinch.

"I do remember that she was not a happy woman," Gunther continued. "No joy in her eyes, or in her voice. The way she would reach for meat. It was as if just the reaching was a burden. As if to lift her arm took all the strength of her soul. I see many people like this, but few as unhappy as her."

"Does this sound right, Calvin?" Lexie asked.

The Schwa shrugged. "I guess."

"Go on," I said. "Tell us about that day."

"Ya, the day." Gunther glanced at the door, to make sure no one would come in to disturb us. "The other butcher who worked here during the day—Oscar was his name—he hated his job. He was a third-generation butcher. In three generations the blood can thin. No passion. No love for the work."

"He couldn't stand the daily grind," said Lexie. I snickered, but quickly shut myself up.

"I never trusted him," Gunther continued. "He was unpredictable. How do you say . . . *impulsive*. He would say such things! He said he would someday slam a cleaver in the manager's desk, and walk out. Or he would threaten to cut the meat into strange, unnatural shapes, just to confuse the customers. I would have to talk him out of such things. He spoke to me of travels he never took to places he wished to go. Alaska, the Florida Keys. Visit the Hopi Indians, kayak the Colorado River. All talk. He never went. Oscar spent his vacations at home alone, and the pressure, it would just build. I didn't know how, I didn't know when, but I knew it was only a matter of time until he snapped. Maybe, I thought, the cleaver would wind up in the manager's head instead of his desk. Or maybe . . . maybe something worse."

"What does this have to do with my mother?" the Schwa asked impatiently.

"Very much to do with your mother," Gunther said. "Because your mother was there when he finally snapped." Gunther leaned forward, looking directly at the Schwa. It was like me and Lexie were no longer in the room.

"Actually," Gunther said, "it was your mother who snapped first. I was right here in the back room when I heard it. This woman crying. Crying like someone had died. Crying like the world had come to an end. I don't do well with crying women. I stayed back. Oscar was the emotional butcher—he was best with the emotional customers, so I let him talk to her.

"First he talked to her over the counter, trying to calm her down. Then he took her behind the counter and sat her down. I had to take over special orders while they talked. I could hear some of what they said. She felt like she was watching her own life from the outside, as if through a spyglass. So did he. Many times she thought she might end it all. So did he. But she never did . . . because more than anything, she was afraid that no one would notice that she was gone."

I could almost see the blood draining from the Schwa's face. He was so pale now I thought he might pass out.

"I go back to fill a special order for lamb shanks. It was the Passover, you know. Never enough lamb shanks at the Passover. When I come back, Oscar has taken off his apron, and he hands it to me. 'I'm going,' he says. 'But Oscar, still you have half an hour of duty,' I tell him. 'Busiest time. And the Passover!' But he doesn't care. 'Tell the manager the beef stops here,' he says. Then he takes your mother's hand, pulls her out of the chair—maybe that same chair you sit in now. He pulls her up, and now she's laughing instead of crying, and then they run out the back way, like two cuckoos in love. That's the last anyone has ever seen of them."

The Schwa stared at him, slack-jawed.

"There you have it," Gunther said, crossing his legs in satisfaction. "Do you want me to tell it again?"

The Schwa's head began to shake, but not in the normal controlled way. It kind of moved like one of those bobble-head dolls. "My mother ran away with the butcher?"

"It is more correct to say that he ran away with her . . . but yes, this is what happened."

His head kept on bobbling. "My mother ran away with the BUTCHER?"

Gunther looked at me, as if I should explain why the Schwa kept repeating the question.

The Schwa was borderline ballistic. "What kind of sick person runs off with a butcher, and leaves her five-year-old kid in the frozen-food section?"

"These are questions I cannot answer," Gunther said.

"The important thing," I told him, "is that she didn't disappear."

"THIS IS WORSE!" he screamed so suddenly it made Gunther jump. "THIS IS WAY WORSE! THE *BUTCHER?*"

He stood up and his chair flew out behind him, hitting a stainless-steel table that rang out like a bell. *"I hate her! I hate her guts! I hate her hate her hate her!"*

Gunther stood and backed away. "Maybe I go finish cleaning." Since emotional customers weren't his thing, he disappeared into the meat locker to hide.

Now it wasn't just the Schwa's head that was shaking, it was his whole body. His fists were clenched and quivering, turning white as his face turned red.

"She left me there, and I thought . . . I thought it was my fault."

"Calvin, it's all right!" said Lexie.

"No, it's not! It's never going to be all right! How could it ever be? How could you even say that?"

And suddenly I began to wonder if maybe knowing the truth was the worst thing for him. Maybe I had made the mother of all mistakes, letting him find out. Which is worse, the friend who keeps the truth secret, or the friend that spills the beans? As Gunther would say, "These are questions I cannot answer." Anyway, I didn't want to think about those questions just then. I knew I'd think about them after I got home, and stay up all night thinking about what a moron I was, and maybe I oughta be made of Pisher Plastic myself, for all the sense I have.

Lexie clasped the Schwa's hands, trying to comfort him, and he just broke down like the five-year-old he once was in that shopping cart. "I hate her," he wailed, but his wails were growing softer. "I hate her . . ."

I put my hand on his shoulder, and squeezed until I felt his shaking begin to fade. "Welcome to the visible world," I told him, gently. "I'm really glad you're here."

We barely spoke once we got back into the car, and although the silence was miserable and uncomfortable, breaking it was harder than you might think. We had the driver drop the Schwa off first, then Lexie, then me, leaving me lots of quality time with myself in the backseat to feel lousy about the whole thing. How could I live with myself if I totally ruined the Schwa's life? What kind of person did that make me? Why did I have to put myself smack in the middle of all of this?

My parents, whose favorite line whenever I showed up late

was, "We were about to call the police," had called the police. When Lexie's driver pulled up to my house, there was an NYPD cruiser out front, its lights spinning, sending kaleidoscope flashes around the street, where neighbors all peered out from behind their blinds. *Great,* I thought. *The perfect way to end this night.* I thanked the driver, then took a deep breath and strode into the house, hoping to come up with something clever to say. But no brilliance introduced itself at the time, so I just walked in, playing clueless, and said, "What's going on?"

The look of despair on my parents' faces was not replaced by fury when they saw me. I wondered why. A cop stood with them between the foyer and the living room. The cop didn't start to wrap everything up when he saw me, either. I wondered about this, too, and began to get that vague, uneasy feeling that maybe they hadn't called the police. Maybe the police came on their own. Then it began to dawn on me that maybe this had nothing to do with me. Suddenly I started to feel my throat begin to tighten, and my skin begin to get hot and squirmy.

"It's Frankie . . ." Mom said.

I didn't want to ask. I didn't want to know. Suddenly I was seeing all the things my mother imagines when one of us is late. I saw Frankie lying in a ditch, I saw him splattered over Nostrand Avenue, I saw him stabbed in an alley. But my parents weren't offering information, so I had to ask.

"What happened to Frankie?"

My parents just looked to each other rather than telling me, so the policeman spoke up instead. "Your brother's been arrested for drunk driving."

I let out a gust of air, just then realizing that I hadn't been breathing.

"He wasn't actually driving," added Mom, talking more to the cop than to me. "He backed the car into a duck pond."

"That's driving," the cop reminded her.

I wanted to tell them that it was impossible—that Frankie didn't drink—I mean, he was the *good* brother, the A student, the perfect son. That's what I wanted to say, but my brain got locked on "stupid," and I said, "Where's there a duck pond in Brooklyn?"

"Is he going to prison?" Christina asked. "Do we have to talk to him through glass?"

"It's his first offense," Dad said. "He'll lose his license for a year, and have to do community service. That's what they gave me when I was his age."

I did a major double take. "You? You mean you got arrested for drunk driving? You never drink and drive!"

"Exactly," Dad said.

Then my mother looked at me, suddenly realizing something. "Where were you? Why are you coming home so late?"

So they hadn't even noticed I was gone. But that was okay. I could live without being the center of attention. I didn't need my face on a billboard, or on a mug shot. And it occurred to me that going unnoticed sometimes meant that you were trusted to do the right thing.

"Don't worry about it," I told them. "You go take care of Frankie."

The Weird Things Kids Do
Don't Even Come Close to
the Weird Things Parents Do

20 The way I see it, truth only looks good when you're looking at it from far away. It's kind of like that beautiful girl you see on the street when you're riding past in the bus, because beautiful people never ride the bus—at least not when I'm on it. Usually I get the people with so much hair in their nose, it looks like they're growing sea urchins in there—or those women with gray hair all teased out so you can see their scalp underneath, making me wonder if I blew on their hair, would it all fly away like dandelion seeds? So you're sitting on the bus and you look out through the dandelion heads, and there she is, this amazing girl walking by on the street, and you think if you could only get off this stupid bus and introduce yourself to her, your life would change.

The thing is, she's not as perfect as you think, and if you ever got off the bus to introduce yourself, you'd find out she's got a fake tooth that's turning a little bit green, breath like a race-horse, and a zit on her forehead that keeps drawing your eyes toward it like a black hole. This girl is truth. She's not so pretty, not so nice. But then, once you get to know her, all that stuff doesn't seem to matter. Except maybe for the breath, but that's why there's Altoids.

The Schwa wanted to know the truth more than anything else in his life. So now he was looking at bad teeth, bad skin, and a funky smell.

I know what happened in my house that night, but what happened in the Schwa's house after he got home I can only imagine. All I know is what happened after. The radioactive fallout, you might say. But I've had plenty of time to imagine it, and I'm pretty sure it went something like this:

The Schwa gets home to find his father sitting up, feeling helpless. He's too much of a wreck even to play guitar, because for once, he's actually noticed that his son wasn't home. Maybe he's even been crying, because the Schwa is more like the father, and he's more like the kid.

The Schwa comes in, sees him there, and offers no explanation. He waits for his father to talk first.

"Where were you, do you have any idea how worried, blah blah blah—"

He lets his dad rant, and when his dad is done, the Schwa, still keeping his hands calmly in his pockets, asks, "Where's Mom?"

His father is thrown. He hesitates, then says, "Never mind that, where were you?"

"Where are Mom's pictures?" the Schwa asks. "I know there must have been pictures. Where are they?"

Now his father's getting scared. Not the same kind of fear he had as he waited for the Schwa to get home, but in its own way just as bad. The Schwa's afraid, too. It's the fear you feel when you're off the bus, standing in front of that beautiful/horrible girl.

"Don't tell me you don't remember," the Schwa says. "Tell me why there aren't any pictures."

"There are pictures," his father finally says. "They're just put away, that's all."

"Why?"

"Because she left us!" he yells.

"She left you!" the Schwa screams back.

"No," his father says, more softly this time. "She left us."

And Calvin, no matter how much he tightens his jaw, he can't deny the ugly green-toothed truth. She left him, too.

They look at each other for a moment. The Schwa knows if it goes on too long, it will end right here. His father will clam up, and everything would go back to the way it was. But Mr. Schwa, to his credit, doesn't wait long enough for that to happen. "Come on," he says, and he leads his son out to the garage.

In the corner of the garage, hidden beneath other junk, is a suitcase. He pulls it out, opens it up, and takes out a shoe box, handing it to the Schwa.

The Schwa is almost afraid to open it, but in the end he does. He has to. Inside he finds envelopes—at least fifty of them. Every one of them is addressed in the same feminine handwriting. None of them have been opened, and all are addressed to the same person.

"These were written to me," he says.

"If she wanted to talk to you, she could have come herself. I told her that."

"You spoke to her?"

"She used to call."

"And you never told me?"

His father's face gets hard. "If she wanted to talk to you," he says again, "she could have come herself."

The Schwa doesn't know which is worse—what his mother did, or what his father had done. She left, yes, but he made her disappear.

"When did the letters start coming?" the Schwa asks.

His father doesn't hold back anything anymore. He couldn't if he tried. "A few weeks after she left."

"And when did the last one come?"

His father doesn't answer right away. It's hard for him to say. Finally he tells him, "I can't remember."

He can't look his son in the face, but the Schwa, he can stare straight at his father, right through him. "I spent our savings to rent a billboard," he tells his father. "A big picture of my face."

The man doesn't understand. "Why?"

"To prove I'm not invisible."

The Schwa does not cry—he is past tears—but his father isn't. The tears roll down the man's face. "You're not invisible, Calvin."

"I wish I had known sooner."

Then the Schwa goes into his room, closes the door, and goes through the letters one by one. Some have return addresses, some don't, but it doesn't matter because the return address is never the same. It's the postmark that tells the best story. Fifty letters at least . . . and almost every postmark is from a different state.

Why I Started Vandalizing Brooklyn

21 The Schwa came to school on Monday with the shoe box of letters. He showed it to me as I stood at my locker before class, but I couldn't read his emotions. He seemed changed in a basic way. You know—it's like how when an egg is boiled it looks the same on the outside, but it's different on the inside. I didn't know what I was looking at now—Schwa, or hard-boiled Schwa.

"Can I read the letters?" I asked.

He held them back. "They were written to me."

"Well, will you at least tell me what she said?"

He thought about the question and shrugged, without looking at me. "Mostly she writes about the places she's been. 'Wish you were here' kind of stuff."

"But . . . did she say why she did it? Why she left?"

The Schwa did that weird not-looking-at-me shrug again. "She talked about it in her early letters. Said she was sorry a lot, and that it had nothing to do with me." But he didn't explain any further. Then he held out an envelope. "This is the most recent one. It's about six months old." I looked at it. The envelope had no return address. "It's from Key West, Florida—see the postmark?"

I tried to peek at the letter, but he pulled it away from me. "I'm going to write back."

"How can you without an address?"

The Schwa shrugged yet again. "Key West isn't all that big. Maybe the post office knows her. And if that doesn't work, I'll find her some other way."

I could have argued how unlikely that was, but who was I to shoot down his dream? If he was able to get himself a paper clip from the *Titanic,* and get his face slapped up on a billboard, maybe he could find his mother. The Schwa was tenacious—a word that I, for once, got right on my vocabulary test.

He took a long look at the handwriting on the letter. "Someday I want to tell her to her face what a lousy thing she did. And I want her to tell me to *my* face that she's sorry."

I closed my locker and spun the lock. "Good luck, Schwa. I really hope you find her." But when I looked at where he was standing, he had already vanished.

When I got home that afternoon, the house was empty. Or so I thought. I passed by my father twice in the living room without even noticing he was there. On the third pass, I noticed him sitting in an armchair, blending into the shadows of the room, staring kind of blankly into space.

"Dad?"

"Hi, Antsy," he said quietly.

"You're home early."

He didn't answer for a while. "Yeah, well, thought I'd take some time off."

There was something off about this. "Work okay?" I asked. "Are you building a better Bullpucky? Manny, I mean."

"Work couldn't be better," he said. "I got fired today."

I chuckled at first, thinking he was making some kind of joke, but he didn't laugh.

"What? You can't be serious!"

"They called it an 'executive offload.'"

"They fired a bunch of you?" I still couldn't believe it. Dad had worked for Pisher since before I could remember.

He shook his head. "Just me."

"Those creeps."

He raised his eyebrows. "They gave me a nice parachute, though."

"Huh?"

"Severance package. Money enough to hold me until I get another job. If I get one."

"Did you tell Mom?"

"No!" he said sharply. "And you don't tell her either. I'll tell her when I'm good and ready."

I was going to ask him why he told me, but stopped myself. I decided just to feel grateful that he did.

I sat down on the couch, feeling awkward about the whole thing, but still not wanting to leave. I offered to get him a beer, but he said no, that he just wanted to sit there for a while getting used to the feeling of being jobless. Like maybe the air might be thinner for the unemployed.

"So what's new with you?" he asked.

"Not a whole lot," I told him. "Remember my friend? The one who's invisible-ish?"

"Vaguely," he said, which was better than "not at all."

I told him the whole story. Everything—from the butcher to the billboard to the box of letters.

"Ran away with the butcher!" Dad said. "Ya gotta love that."

"So, was letting him know the right thing to do?"

He thought about it. "Probably," he said. "Did you do it because you wanted to tell him, or because he needed to hear it?"

I didn't even have to think about the answer to that one. "He needed to hear it. Definitely."

"So your intentions were good. That's what matters."

"But isn't, like, the road to hell paved with good intentions?"

"Yeah, well, so's the road to heaven. And if you spend too much time thinking about where those good intentions are taking you, you know where you end up?"

"Jersey?"

"I was thinking 'nowhere,' but you get the point." The expression on his faced darkened again. I could tell he was thinking about work.

"I'm really sorry about your job," I told him.

"I was just fired from a company whose biggest contribution to civilization is a urinal strainer," he said. "That's nothing to feel sorry about." He smiled as he thought about it, then shook his head. "Although sometimes I wonder if 'the Man Upstairs' is working me over for something I did."

The Man Upstairs, I thought, and something began to trouble me. Because I knew a man upstairs, too.

"Uh . . . Dad. What reason did they give for firing you?"

"It was the weirdest thing. They gave me this story about

someone making a massive investment in our product development, but only if they fired *me*."

I suddenly felt my skin begin to pull tight, like shrink-wrap on the Night Butcher's steaks.

"It doesn't make sense," he said. "Why would anyone do that?"

Someone gave a ton of money . . . but only if my dad was fired. There was only one person I knew twisted enough to do something like that. Someone who had made a threat to get my dad fired once before.

When I got to Crawley's place, the old man didn't seem surprised to see me. That was my first clue that my suspicions were right on target.

"I need someone to walk my dogs," he said as he opened the door.

"I couldn't care less," I told him. "You got my dad fired, didn't you, you twisted old—"

"Careful, Mr. Bonano. I don't take kindly to crude insults."

I paced away from him, my fists clenched. Controlling your temper isn't easy when you really don't want to control it. If I blew a gasket now, though, I knew it could be a whole lot worse. This guy could end up punishing my whole family for the things I did.

"You're a monster," I told him. "My father worked nine years for that company, and now what is he going to do?"

He calmly returned to his place on the living-room sofa. "Why is that my problem?"

I felt like charging at him, but instead let loose a scream of pure rage that got all the dogs barking. And when the dogs quieted down, Crawley said, "Perhaps I can offer him some menial position." He gave me the nastiest of smirks. "Floor scrubber . . . janitor . . . dog walker."

I was about to tell him exactly what he could do with his menial position, but then he said, "Of course there *is* that new restaurant I recently acquired . . ." He looked off, scratching his temple like this was something that just occurred to him, when clearly it wasn't.

"What are you talking about?"

"I've decided one restaurant isn't enough, so I bought a second one a few miles away. An Italian place."

"My father is not sweeping your floors!"

"No, I don't expect he would." Crawley looked at me, dragging this out like a sick kid pulling the wings off a fly. "What I really need is a business partner for the new restaurant. Someone who can run it. Someone who knows Italian cooking."

I tried to speak, but all that came out was a stuttering, "Duh . . . duh . . . duh."

"Do you know of anyone in need of employment who might fit those qualifications?"

"H-h-how much does it pay?"

Crawley grinned like the Grinch. "Certainly more than Pisher Plastics."

How was I supposed to respond to this? Did Crawley get my father fired just so he could offer him what he always wanted? How twisted is that? It's like the guy who throws somebody overboard just so he can rescue him and be the big hero. Crawley was so good at pulling strings, and at underhanded manipulation. Did I want my father under Crawley's thumb? And then I realized with a little bit of relief that it wasn't my decision to make. It was my father's.

"Tell him to pay me a visit," Crawley said.

"Yeah," I said. "Yeah, sure." I turned to go, in a bit of a daze. All that was left of my anger was a whole lot of smoke for me to choke on. But before I escaped, Crawley stopped me.

"One more thing. I have a job for you, too."

"Walking dogs?"

'No." He grabbed his cane, stood up, and crossed the room toward me. "I understand that you are no longer dating my granddaughter."

"Yeah, so?"

"I would like you to pretend that you are when her parents return from Europe."

"Excuse me?"

"You see, her parents absolutely despise you, so that makes you my best friend."

"How can they despise me? They've never even met me!"

"They despise the *concept* of you."

There are a whole lot of things about rich people I don't think I'll ever understand. But somehow I think it's better that way. "I don't want to be paid to date Lexie, so keep your money in your grubby little hands where it belongs."

"That's not the job I'm talking about." He took another step closer, and for the first time, I sensed in him just a little bit of uncertainty. He squinted, like he was examining me, but I could tell he was deciding whether or not to offer me this "job" at all.

"For the monthly stipend of one hundred dollars, plus expenses, I would like you and my granddaughter to kidnap me once each month."

"Excuse me?"

"You heard me," he snapped. "You are to kidnap me. You are to catch me by surprise. You are to plan some creative and adventurous event. And if I don't threaten to have you jailed at least once during the day, then you shall be fired."

Then he turned around and went back to the sofa, refusing to look at me again.

"Kidnap you, huh? I woulda done that for free."

"Telling me that is bad business," he grunted. "Now leave."

Even before I mentioned it to my father, I called the Schwa. He knew Crawley—he'd be able to commiserate. But when I dial his number, I get this recording. The number's been disconnected. At first I thought it must be a mistake, so I dialed again, and got the same thing. There was no forwarding number.

The feeling I had deep down in my gut was even worse than what I felt when my dad told me how he got fired. It was sundown now. Flurries were falling, and the wind had gotten blizzard cold. Still, I got on my bike and rode at full speed to the Schwa's house.

There was a FOR SALE sign on the lawn.

It had red lettering and featured the picture of a realtor, her face grinning out at me. Rona Josephson, million-dollar seller. I had never met the woman, but I already hated her.

I hurried up to the Schwa's front door, knocked, and didn't wait for an answer before I tried the knob. It was locked. I peeked in the little window next to the door, and my worst fear was confirmed. I didn't see any furniture. I went around the house, looking in every window. The place had been emptied out. There wasn't even any of the usual junk left in corners when you move—the entire place was clean.

I was scared now, the way you're scared when you come home to find someone's broken in and stolen your stuff. I took down the number of the realtor and left. I don't carry a cell phone, because my parents told me I'd have to pay for it myself, and there's no one I'd pay to talk to. The nearest set of pay phones was by the gas station a few blocks away. Four phones. One had a jammed coin slot, two had no receivers, and the last one was hogged by some guy telling his life story. When he saw me coming, he turned his back to me, making it clear he wasn't giving up the phone. It was only when I started hanging around his car, trying to look as suspicious as possible, that I got off the phone and left.

I fed whatever change I had in my pocket into the phone and dialed the realtor's number. A receptionist put me through to Rona Josephson, million-dollar seller.

"I'm calling about a house for sale. I don't want to buy it, I just need to get in touch with the people selling it." Then I gave her the address.

"I'm sorry," she said, not sounding sorry at all, "we can't give out that kind of information."

"I don't care! I need the phone number!"

"Don't you take that tone of voice with me! Who do you think you are?"

This was not going well. I took a deep breath and tried to pretend I wasn't talking to an imbecile. "I'm sorry. The kid who lived there, he . . . he's a friend and, uh . . . he left his medicine in my house. But now I don't know where he is. I have to get him back his medicine."

Silence on the other end. I could almost hear the wheels turning in her little realtor's brain.

"Do you really want to be responsible for him not getting his medication, Miss Josephson?"

More silence. I heard her clicking on her computer, then flipping pages in a notebook. "It says here the property is being sold by a Mrs. Margaret Taylor. The address is in Queens, but I can't quite read my assistant's writing."

"That can't be right. What about Schwa? Somebody named Schwa should be selling it."

"Sorry, it's Taylor." I heard more flipping pages. "And my assistant's notes seem to indicate it has been vacant for months, so you obviously have the wrong house."

Now it was my turn to be silent. I could hear the gears turning in my own brain, and I didn't like it at all.

A recording broke in, announcing that I needed another twenty-five cents to continue the call.

"Hello, are you there?" asked Rona Josephson, million-dollar seller.

"No," I said. "I'm not." And hung up.

At first I was freaked, then I was mad. So the Schwa finally did it. He not only disappeared, but he became like a black hole, sucking in his father, too, and everything they owned. I was going to call Lexie, but I didn't have any more change. What was the point anyway—she would just tell me what she always told me: "There's got to be a rational explanation." But what if there wasn't? And what if when I called Lexie, she said, "Calvin who?" What if I was the only person left who remembered him—and what if I woke up tomorrow morning and didn't remember him either?

No! It wouldn't happen. I would not allow it to happen, but I didn't see how I had any choice in the matter. If the Schwa was right, and he was destined to disappear from memory, what could I do to change that?

As for what I did next, it came, as most of the world's great ideas do, while I was on the can. Maybe the shock of the Schwa's vanishing act did something to my insides, but whatever it was, there was no way I was making it home on a bicycle without a pit stop. So there I am in the stall at Fuggettaburger, trying not to look at the Pisher toilet-paper dispenser, and I catch sight of the things people have scrawled into the wall. The stuff you usually find on the walls of a bathroom is about as Neanderthal as you can get—which is why we often call the boys' bathroom at school the Wendell Tiggor Reading Room. The Fuggettaburger bathroom had its share of unreadable phone numbers, and poems that started, *Here I sit, broken-hearted.* Then, suddenly, as I'm looking at all this drivel, I get an uncontrollable urge to put something up there myself. I take a pen from my jacket pocket, and I start scratching a picture onto the wall. I'm not on the short list when it comes to artistic talent, but I can do faces okay. So I draw this face. Just a few simple lines, wispy hair. Then beneath it I write, *The Schwa Was Here.* And, for a final touch, right on his forehead, I draw an upside down *e*—you know, like a schwa in the dictionary.

Just like that.

By the time I leave Fuggettaburger, I'm a man with a mission. I went down the street to the pharmacy and bought myself one of those black permanent markers. Not the skinny kind, but the real thick ones. I drew the same thing right over a bus-stop billboard, only this time it was with much thicker lines. I did it on a park bench. I got on the subway and put Schwas inside as many cars as I could. A few people made noises. Mumbled words like "vandal" and stuff like that, but I just ignored them, because I knew this wasn't graffiti. This wasn't tagging. That's all about making your mark and labeling territory. I was making someone else's mark. *The Schwa Was Here.* I didn't care if people saw me, I didn't care if I got caught, because what I was doing was noble, and God help anyone who tried to stop me.

That day I must have put up maybe a hundred Schwas all over Brooklyn, and when I finally got home, my hand was covered in black ink. I felt like I had run a marathon—that feeling of exhaustion and incredible accomplishment all rolled together.

It was past eleven, and my mother was waiting at the door. "Where were you?" she yelled. "We almost called the police."

"I was vandalizing bus stops and public restrooms," I said. She grounded me until the fall of civilization, and I took it like a man.

Dad was sitting in the living room watching TV, with Christina dozing in his lap. Frankie was asleep after a day of community service. I told my dad he should give Old Man Crawley a call. I told him it was important. He gave me that "what?" expression, and I gave him that "don't ask me" look.

When I got to my room, I didn't go to sleep. I knew what

I had to do. I got online and pulled up the Queens phone book. Margaret Taylor. She was the person selling the house. There were fifty-six Margaret Taylors in Queens, and two hundred sixty-seven M. Taylors. The next morning, I began making calls.

My Anonymous Contribution
to Popular Culture and to
My Parents' Phone Bill

22 *"Hello, is this Margaret Taylor?"*
"Yes, this is she."
"Are you selling a house in Brooklyn?"
"Brooklyn? No, I'm sorry."
"Okay. Thanks anyway."

The Schwa didn't show up the next week, or the next, or the next. I wasn't surprised. I went to the attendance office to check if his school records had been transferred, but someone had misplaced his entire file. That didn't surprise me either. What surprised me was the Schwa face I saw drawn in the Wendell Tiggor Reading Room. It looked like the faces I had drawn around town, but I hadn't drawn one in this bathroom. Plus, *The Schwa Was Here* was written in a handwriting that didn't look like mine at all.

"Hello, I'm calling for Margaret Taylor."
"You found her. What can I do for you?"
"I hear you're selling a house in Brooklyn."

"Honey, if I owned a house anywhere, I wouldn't be selling it."

I dreamed about the Schwa one night. In the dream I was standing in the middle of Times Square. A bus goes by, and on the side of the bus, instead of an advertisement for a Broadway show, it's a picture of the Schwa. I look at a bus stop—there he is again. I look up in the sky, he's on the Goodyear Blimp—and finally the giant electronic billboard overlooking Times Square has him on a live video feed.

"Antsy!" the Schwa yells down from the giant screen. "Antsy—tell them to look! Make them look at me, Antsy!" I glance around, and even though there's like fourteen thousand people hurrying by, not one of them is looking at the billboards. "Make them look, Antsy! Make them look!"

Then suddenly I'm standing inside the gondola of the Goodyear Blimp, and the New York Jets are there. So's Darth Vader. You know how dreams are.

I rode the bus to school that day, thinking about the dream. There were no advertisements featuring the Schwa on the bus to school, or on the bus home. But on the way home, I caught sight of something strange. It was snowing. Just a dusting, really. The kind of stuff that sticks, but doesn't hang around till morning. You might be able to scrape a snowball or two off a cold car hood, but it's not worth the effort.

So I'm looking out of the window of the bus, thinking about Lexie, and how her parents were due home any day, and wondering if they might send her to some private school on an uncharted island to get her away from me, when all of a sudden I see a schwa drawn in the thin layer of snow on the back window of a parked Chevy. I get out at the next stop and go back to find it, but by the time I get there, the car's gone.

"Hello, I'd like to speak to M. Taylor."

"Speaking. Who's this?"

"Sorry, sir. Wrong number."

My mother thought I was nuts, the way I spent an hour every evening making these calls. She thought I must have been driven temporarily insane by puberty, or something. In addition to giving me zits and body odor, it made me a phone freak. The way I saw it, though, it was a kind of a penance. My personal punishment for taking advantage of the Schwa the way I did when we first discovered the Schwa Effect, and for pushing him away because I wanted to be the one dating Lexie. And for not taking him to the Night Butcher before he blew all that money on the billboard. Picking up that phone and calmly dialing one stranger after another was like some weird badge of honor. It became a part of my daily routine—something I did without thinking—like the way I would look for schwas drawn in new places each time I went out. I was finding a lot of them. Christina must have seen them, too, because she drew one on her lunch box. I couldn't explain it any more than I could explain why I felt compelled to make those calls every day.

"Hi, is this M. Taylor?"

"Yes."

"The 'M' doesn't stand for Margaret, does it?"

"Well, yes, it does. Can I help you?"

"Probably not. You're not selling a house in Brooklyn are you?"

"Why? Are you interested? It's in excellent condition!"

I nearly had a coronary on the spot. I had never gotten this far before. I was so used to hanging up, I didn't even know what to say next.

"Hello?" she said. "Are you there?"

"Yeah, yeah. Listen, I'm looking for someone who lived there. A kid named Calvin Schwa."

"Oh, are you one of his friends?"

Again nothing but dead air on my end of the line. It then occurred to me that this was the infamous Aunt Peggy. Don't ask me what imbecile decided Peggy was short for Margaret. I was feeling kind of rubber-brained. It's like when you call the radio station when they ask for the ninth caller, but you're never the ninth caller, so when they actually pick up and talk to you, you figure it must be some mistake. Then they put you on the radio, you sound like a complete fool, and then you hang up before you can give them your address, so they can't mail you your concert tickets. Don't laugh—it happened.

"Yeah, I'm a friend," I told Aunt Peggy. "Is he there? Can I talk to him?"

"I'm afraid he isn't here. I could take a message, though."

"Well, could you tell me why he moved like that? And why you're selling his house?"

I heard Aunt Peggy sigh. "I probably shouldn't be telling you this, but I suppose it's common knowledge by now. They were having trouble with finances," she told me. "And Calvin's father, well, he doesn't handle this sort of thing well. I put the house up for sale for him, and he moved in with me."

"Will Calvin be back later tonight? I really need to talk to him."

"Oh, he didn't come here with his father," Aunt Peggy said. "He stayed with a friend in Brooklyn so he could finish out the school year."

"Great—could you give me the number?"

"Of course. His name is Anthony Bonano. If you hold on, I'll get the number."

I pulled the phone away from my ear, and looked at it like it had suddenly turned into a banana.

"Hello?" said Aunt Peggy. "Are you still there? Do you want that number?"

"Uh . . . That's okay," I said. "Never mind." I hung up and stared at the phone for a full minute. It was then that I finally decided to just let this be. So, the Schwa had disappeared, but like his mother, it was completely of his own doing. It might have been misguided like so many things he did, but I had to respect his decision, and although I had a sneaking suspicion what he was up to, I wasn't about to hunt him down. I had already done my penance.

The Schwa never came back to Brooklyn, and life went on without him. Lexie's parents returned from their European spree, and just as Crawley said, they hated my guts, which really wasn't a problem, since I'm fairly used to people hating my guts.

"They're convinced anyone with the last name Bonano has to have Mafia ties," Lexie told me, which is like saying anyone named Simpson is either related to Homer or O.J.

"Let 'em think that," I told her. "They'll be afraid to piss me off." Which I think is why they don't say boo when I'm around. It turns out that fake-dating Lexie felt a lot like the real thing, without all that boyfriend-girlfriend pressure.

As for Crawley, he did find himself another pair of dog walkers: Howie and Ira—who I think keep hoping another couple of granddaughters will turn up.

"You'll like Howie," I told Crawley. "He's like a Rubik's Cube with every side the same color."

When they first showed up, Howie begins this discussion with Crawley about the dog's names. "They're named after the seven deadly sins and seven virtues," Crawley tells him.

Howie considers this deeply, then says, "Why not the four freedoms?"

"That," says Crawley, "would leave ten dogs unnamed."

Howie raises his eyebrows. "Not if you named the rest after the Bill of Rights."

Crawley goes red in the face with anger, Ira gets it on film, and their relationship is off to a flying start.

My father was too proud to call Crawley right away. He looked for work for about six weeks, then finally made the phone call and took a meeting with Old Man Crawley. He returned from Crawley's in shell shock, but with a job. Well, more than just a job. The old hermit crab made my father a partner in his new restaurant. He let my dad turn it into whatever he wanted, and in true Crawley fashion, he threatened my father with everything short of eternal damnation if the restaurant ever failed. Dad, in his wisdom, decided to get Mom into it, too, turning it into a combination Italian-French place. They named it Paris, *capisce*? and so far, so good.

There are schwas drawn in the restaurant's bathrooms that I didn't put there.

In fact, there are schwas everywhere now. I got a call from Ira during spring break. He was on vacation in Hawaii, and he called to tell me he saw one scribbled across a DANGER, HOT LAVA sign. They've got them clear across the country—maybe clear around the world. There's got to be hundreds of people doing it. No one knows who draws them, or why, but now they're a they're a permanent part of the landscape. Howie has a theory that involves aliens and cosmic string theory, but trust me, you don't want to hear it.

The Schwa Was Here. Just a few of us know what it really means, and nobody believes me when I tell them that I started it. But that's okay. I can handle being anonymous.

As for the Schwa himself, I never saw him again—but I did get a letter. It came in August, more than six months after he pulled his disappearing act.

> *Dear Antsy,*
>
> *I guess you thought I vanished into thin air, huh? Did you freak? You're smart, though, you probably figured out where I went—and guess what? I found her! My mom was in Florida after all. I got to Key West just as she was getting ready to move on. I told her she owed me big, and she agreed, so she took me along with her. She's not what I expected. She knows lots of stuff. She even taught me to scuba dive—and I can get really close to the fish because—get this— they don't notice I'm there.*
>
> *Say hello to everyone for me. I won't forget you if you promise not to forget me!*
>
> *Your friend,*
> *Calvin*

Clipped to the letter was a photo of the Schwa and his mom on a tropical beach. She didn't look like the unhappy woman the

Night Butcher had described. The Schwa almost had a tan in the picture, if you can believe that, and he had a smile on his face as wide as the one on his billboard.

I had to smile, too. The postmark was from Puerto Rico, but the paper clip had been to the moon.

Thə End

Neal Shusterman's novels have been honored with awards from the International Reading Association, the American Library Association, and readers in many states. His novels span several genres, from humor to suspense thrillers to science fiction.

Of *The Schwa Was Here*, he says: "The idea came to me in the middle of an author visit. I was answering questions in a school library when a teacher pointed out a boy who had had his hand up the whole time, and I hadn't noticed. He was sitting in front of the library's big dictionary, and I made this odd connection: The kid was unnoticeable—like a 'schwa' in the dictionary." Mr. Shusterman lives in Southern California with his four children. Visit his Web site at www.storyman.com